The Ve

Deception

And

The Lady Swindlers

1

Dedication.

For my family and friends, who have shared in my laughter, dried my tears, and celebrated every minor victory along the way. Your presence in my life is a gift, and your support has been invaluable in bringing this book to fruition. This is for you.

Step into the glittering, treacherous world of Regency London, where appearances are everything and a whispered secret can shatter a reputation. *'The Velvet Deception and the Lady Swindlers'* invites you on a thrilling journey through the opulent ballrooms and shadowed alleyways of 18th-century England, a time when ambition knew no bounds and cunning was the ultimate currency.

While this novel is set against the backdrop of the Regency era, please be advised that *'The Velvet Deception'* is a work of *'historical fiction'*. The characters you encounter – from the enigmatic Seraphina Vance and her loyal accomplice Aron, to the relentless Bow Street magistrate Thomas Garrick and the tragically misguided Colette Delacroix – are entirely products of my imagination. Similarly, the daring plots, the intricate swindles, and the dramatic events that unfold within these pages are purely fictional and designed to entertain.

Prepare to be swept away by a tale of ambition, betrayal, and the art of the perfect illusion, where the line between hero and villain is as exquisitely blurred as the mists over the Thames. Enjoy the deception....

Sonia Jones

The year I was born, 1785, was a lifetime away from the velvet drawing-rooms I now frequented. My first breaths were drawn in the festering alleys of St. Giles, a London rookery where the air was thick with the stench of poverty and desperation. My earliest memories are a blur of grey: the permanent damp of cobbled streets, the hollow ache in my belly, the constant, low hum of fear. My mother, a phantom of a woman broken by consumption, clung to life in a single, shared room, her cough a constant, rattling symphony. She died when I was barely five, leaving me to the tender mercies of the streets.

I learned to survive by my wits, a constant, gnawing hunger; my only tutor. I became quick and possessed a pair of eyes that saw everything and betrayed nothing. I knew the best corners for begging, the quickest routes to disappear into the teeming crowds, the faces that promised a copper and those that promised only pain. Theft became an art, a necessity. A purloined loaf of bread, a dropped coin, a silk handkerchief snatched from a gentleman's pocket – these were my daily triumphs. I was a gutter rat, insignificant, invisible, one of a thousand lost souls scrambling for crumbs in the sprawling maw of London.

My tenth year brought with it a harsh winter, colder and crueller than any I had known. The river Thames itself began to freeze, and the usual scraps of food vanished. I huddled in a doorway, shivering, my fingers numb with cold, when the carriage stopped.

It was a sleek, black vehicle, unlike any I had ever seen in the Rookery, and the woman who emerged from it was a vision.

She moved with a grace that bordered on sovereign—her cloak a cascade of midnight, her eyes glinting with a sharp, unsettling clarity even in the gloom. I didn't know her name then, only the chill she carried like perfume. Madam Colette Delacroix. It would be whispered to me later, like a secret too potent to speak aloud.

She studied me—not with pity, not with revulsion, but with a gaze that sliced through grime and fear. Calculating. Precise.

"You, girl," she said, her voice a velvet drawl, smooth and dangerous as the silk that clung to her frame. "You have quick eyes. And hunger."

I recoiled, instinct twitching toward escape. But her stare pinned me, not with threat, but with promise. Something unspoken passed between us—an invitation that reached beyond the filth and scraps of the alley.

She chose me. And two others. Girls like me, scraped from the same guttered existence. We trembled, confused, afraid. But beneath the terror, something stirred. A fragile ember. Hope, perhaps. Or something darker.

Colette took us to her establishment, a grand house in a respectable, though discreet, part of town. It was her brothel, yes, but it was also her academy. We were cleaned, fed, clothed in soft linens, and given a bed that didn't share space with vermin. The transformation was startling. But the true education began after the initial shock wore off.

Colette saw not just a desperate child, but raw potential. She had an uncanny eye for it, for the flash of intelligence, the spark of ambition, the ability to observe and adapt. She taught us to speak properly, smoothing the rough edges of our street dialects until we could mimic the lilting accents of the gentry. She taught us history, literature, music — not for the sake of knowledge, but as tools, as conversational weapons. We trained in the art of deportment until our movements were as fluid as water, our gestures as elegant as any debutante's. We learned to dance, to play the pianoforte; to master the intricate art of social graces.

But most importantly, Colette taught us the art of the swindle. Her brothel was merely a façade, a convenient cover for her true enterprise. She recognised that the greatest wealth lay not in the bodies of men, but in their greed, their vanity, their carefully guarded secrets. She taught us to listen, to observe, to charm. To identify weaknesses, to spin plausible tales, to manipulate without ever raising suspicion. We became adept at cardsharping, at conning dissolute young lords out of their allowances, at orchestrating elaborate schemes that often left our targets none the wiser, only poorer.

"A true lady swindler," Colette would often say, her eyes gleaming, "does not take by force. She takes it by invitation. She makes them want to

give it to her by making them believe it is their own cleverness that has gained them something of value, when in truth, they have lost everything."

She showed us how to dress not just elegantly, but strategically. How to use a fan to convey a thousand meanings. How a well-placed whisper could ignite a scandal or secure a fortune. She honed our instincts, turning the street smarts that had kept me alive into the refined tools of a sophisticated manipulator.

The gutter was a distant memory, replaced by the blinding lights of a glittering stage. Colette had hauled me out, not for my sake, but for her own keen vision of what I could be.

She'd painstakingly crafted me into Seraphina, a creature of exquisite charm and dangerous deception, capable of captivating dukes and outwitting the sharpest connoisseurs.

But after years of being her *"Diamond,"* the shine wore off. Her cruelty was a blade, and when some of the other girls went missing for daring to disobey, I knew it was time to make plans to leave…

Chapter 1

Colette Delacroix

The night clung to Paris like a velvet shroud, thick with the damp breath of the Seine and the teeming life of a thousand cobblestone streets. It was the kind of sultry, oppressive darkness that made even the gas lamps in Madame Colette Delacroix's establishment seem to weep. The year was 1810, the very heart of Napoleonic France, a time of Imperial grandeur and whispered intrigues, of dazzling salons and shadowed alleyways. And tucked away discreetly, almost innocuously, in a quiet cul-de-sac just off the bustling Rue de Rivoli, Colette's *'Hotel particulier'* pulsed with a diverse kind of life.

To the casual observer, it was a respectable lodging house, a haven for discerning gentlemen. But step across its threshold, and the illusion dissolved, replaced by a symphony of whispered indiscretions, the low hum of hushed conversations, and the delicate, continuous clinking of crystal glasses. Inside, Colette's house was a finely tuned machine, not of polite society, but of illicit pleasures, of secrets bought and sold, and of expertly executed thievery. And at its very heart, its undisputed, and often ruthless, conductor, was Madame Colette Delacroix herself.

Her smile could be a silken snare, her eyes, dark and knowing, missed nothing, and in her establishment, fortunes could be made and lost, reputations ruined, and priceless jewels vanish as if into thin air. Welcome to Colette's house of pleasure. But be warned, what you find within its walls might just cost you everything.

Upstairs, in a room that smelled faintly of lavender and a more potent, cloying scent of desperation, Seraphina traced the faded outline of a damask rose on the silken wallpaper. Her fingers, still graceful despite years of rough use, still calloused from the intricate dance of picking pockets and nimble from unclasping diamond necklaces, trembled almost imperceptibly. For fifteen long years, she had been one of Madame Colette's most prized assets: a beauty with an innocent, disarming face that could melt the suspicions of the wariest marks, a ghost-swift thief, and, when the occasion demanded it, a courtesan. Each night was a meticulously choreographed performance, a dangerous ballet between calculated seduction and precise larceny. And each morning, as the first grey light of dawn filtered through the tall, grimy Parisian windows, it brought with it a fresh, bitter wave of resentment.

But Seraphina was utterly bone-deep tired of the gilded cage she inhabited, tired of the forced smiles plastered onto her aching face, tired of the knowing, predatory looks that followed her every move. She was weary of the endless, faceless parade of men whose pockets she emptied with skilful ease, and whose base desires she feigned to satisfy with a sigh. But most of all, a cold, simmering fury pulsed within her at the thought of Colette. The Madame's iron grip was tightening, squeezing the very life from Seraphina's soul. Her demands grew more brazen; her punishments, for even the slightest perceived transgression, more swift and brutally severe. Seraphina had witnessed firsthand what happened to girls who dared to cross Colette, and the thought sent a visceral chill, colder than any Parisian fog, spiralling through her. Escape, she knew, was a fleeting dream, a dangerous whisper in the dark. But the alternative was a slow, painful suffocation of her spirit.

Tonight, however, would be different. Tonight, the performance was for herself. She had been meticulously planning, watching, waiting. Colette, for all her cunning, had grown complacent, secure in her dominion. Seraphina knew where the Madame kept her true nest egg, not in some bank or hidden vault, but tucked away in a false bottom of an old writing desk in her private study – a substantial sum, enough to buy Seraphina a new life, far from the smoky drawing rooms and shadowed alleyways of Paris.

A carriage rumbled past outside, shaking the very foundations of the house. Seraphina drew a deep, shaky breath. As the city outside hummed with a thousand secrets, but none as vital, as terrifying, as the one she was about to enact. The moment had come. The money was within reach. And freedom was just a heartbeat away.

The clock on the mantelpiece in Colette's study chimed two bells, echoing through the silent house. Seraphina moved like a wraith, her soft kid slippers making no sound on the Oriental rug. The study was opulent, cloyingly so, with heavy velvet curtains and a scent of expensive brandy and Colette's signature narcissus perfume. Her eyes, however, went straight to the large mahogany writing desk, an imposing piece that dominated one wall.

Her heart hammered against her ribs, a frantic drumbeat against the silence. She'd observed Colette enough times to know the routine, the subtle push of a hidden lever, the faint click of the false bottom. Her fingers, usually so precise, fumbled for a moment before finding the mechanism. With a soft groan of aged wood, a narrow compartment beneath the main drawer sprang open.

Inside, nestled amongst ledgers and a small, silver-backed mirror, were stacks of banknotes, tied with silk ribbons. English pounds, French francs, Dutch guilders – a fortune that represented years of Colette's exploitation. Seraphina didn't count; she simply scooped the bundles, cramming them into a worn leather satchel she'd brought, along with a handful of small, personal keepsakes she'd managed to hide over the years: a tarnished silver locket with a faded miniature, a small, smooth river stone, and a single, well-thumbed book of poetry. She left behind everything else, the fine dresses, the trinkets, the life that wasn't hers.

The satchel was surprisingly heavy, a testament to the weight of her newfound freedom. She slipped out of the study; the door closing with an almost imperceptible click. The grand staircase loomed, but Seraphina knew a servant's passage, a narrow, winding route used for deliveries and discreet exits. She navigated the darkened corridors with the instinct of a seasoned phantom; each floorboard creak, each distant snore, a potential alarm. Then, in an instant, she was outside.

The Parisian night, thick and damp, embraced her, a stark liberation from the stifling warmth of Colette's house. In the deserted cul-de-sac, gas lamps cast long, wavering shadows, flickering against her resolve.

Seraphina drew a breath—ragged, dry, tasting of dust and the faint, metallic tang of freedom. It scraped her throat like the first gasp after drowning. She clutched her plain dark cloak tighter, fingers trembling as they gripped the worn fabric. It was no longer a garment, but a barrier, a talisman against the chill of the Parisian night and the ghosts she carried.

Behind her loomed the house. Not a home, never that. It had been her prison, her theatre, her gilded masquerade. She did not look back. She dared not. To glance over her shoulder would be to invite its claws to drag her back into velvet-lined captivity. Her feet—once trained to glide, to seduce, to obey—now pounded the cobblestones with raw urgency. Each step was a defiance, a declaration. The rhythm she struck was not elegant, but primal. A fugitive's heartbeat resonant through the sleeping streets.

The city did not notice her. Paris, vast and indifferent, swallowed her like rain into its gutters. She became shadow—fluid, fleeting—slipping through alleys and under gaslight, a whisper of silk and resolve. Seraphina Blackwood, once the Lady of the Larceny; now just a name she carried like a blade. She was no longer a spectacle. She was a secret.

Her destination was the void. No safe-house, no plan. Just the open wound of possibility. It terrified her. It thrilled her. The future stretched before her like a blank canvas, trembling with potential and peril. But even the darkest road was brighter than the cage she'd left behind. And so, she ran. Into the ink of the night. Into the unknown. Into herself.

For the first time in fifteen years, Seraphina was not owned, not watched, not choreographed. She was free. Terribly, gloriously free.

The city closed around her, and the chapter of her captivity ended—not with a scream, but with the soft, defiant footfall of a woman reclaiming her fate…

Chapter 2

The Covent Garden Mirage

Five years had passed since Seraphina, a mere whisper of a woman then, had slipped through the oppressive grasp of Madame Colette Delacroix's shadowy employ in Paris. That escape had been a ballet of daring and desperate fortune – a moonless night, a disguised passage on a fishing trawler across a choppy Channel, and a clandestine arrival in the sprawling, indifferent heart of London. It had been a brutal severing, a leap of faith into the unknown, but those five years had been a testament to her relentless will, forging a new life of remarkable independence.

The year was now 1815, and her charming home, nestled discreetly on the fringes of Covent Garden, served as both a sanctuary and a discreet command centre. Aron, her loyal accomplice, as steadfast and reliable as the ancient London plane trees that lined her street, stood always by her side. Together, they were a formidable pair, their wits as sharp as their perfectly tailored suits, their instincts honed by years of living on the knife-edge of legality, and their eyes ever fixed on the horizon, ever prepared for the next audacious venture. The ghosts of Paris still lingered, faint as a lavender scent, but here, in London, Seraphina Vance was mistress of her own destiny.

Now, a new scheme was unfurling, a masterpiece of deception designed to shake the very foundations of the art world: *"The Covent Garden Mirage."* Seraphina envisioned an art exhibition, a glittering facade behind which a high-stakes scam would play out, a symphony of allure and artifice. Her mind, a labyrinth of cunning, was already mapping out every contingency, every feigned smile, every whispered promise. The canvas of her ambition was vast, the brushstrokes bold and precise.

Aron, ever the rationalist, diligently sorted through the latest auction house catalogues, a crease forming between his brows. *"The 'Sleeping Venus'* by Dubois," he murmured, his finger tracing the finely rendered illustration. "They value it at a staggering twenty thousand pounds. Quite the attraction for our collection; wouldn't you agree, Seraphina?"

Seraphina, perched on the arm of a velvet armchair, with a half-smile playing on her lips, merely nodded. "Perfect. The more audacious, the more believable. We'll need a venue that screams opulence, Aron. Something that will make even the most jaded critics feel a tremor of awe."

Their eyes met, a silent understanding passing between them. This wasn't just about the money; it was about the thrill of the chase, the intellectual chess match, the exquisite satisfaction of outsmarting the unsuspecting elite. The Covent Garden Mirage was more than a scam; it was a performance, and Seraphina, the maestro, was ready to take centre stage. The curtain was about to rise, and Covent Garden, with its vibrant history and hidden corners, was about to become the backdrop for their grand illusion.

The air in Seraphina's elegant sitting room was thick with the scent of old paper and fresh coffee as she and Aron delved into the meticulous art of planning. Sunlight streamed through the sash windows, illuminating dust motes dancing in the air, a stark contrast to the shadowy manoeuvres unfolding within.

"The venue is paramount," Seraphina reiterated, her gaze fixed on a map of Covent Garden spread across the antique mahogany table. "It needs to exude old-world charm, yet possess the infrastructure for a modern, high-profile exhibition. Something with a history, a whisper of prestige." Aron, always one step ahead, gestured to a highlighted circle on the map.

"I've been making investigations regarding the rooms at the 'Freemasons Hall' on Great Queen Street," Aron announced, his voice crisp as he consulted his leather-bound notes. "It's a structure of considerable age and distinction, Seraphina. The interiors boast noble and classical grandeur, with soaring ceilings and ornate plasterwork. I am told it has hosted the most significant assemblies—from royal patronage to grand public exhibitions. Its prime situation, connecting Covent Garden to Holborn, is unrivalled. It practically screams legitimacy."

Seraphina's eyes, sharp and intelligent, gleamed with approval. "Excellent, Aron. That's precisely the kind of sobriety we need. It'll lend an air of undeniable authenticity to our… 'curated' collection." She leant back in her chair, a thoughtful, almost predatory, expression settling on her face. "Now, for the collection itself. The *Sleeping Venus* is, of course, a magnificent anchor. But we need a supporting cast. Pieces that are valuable enough to attract serious collectors, yet obscure enough that their provenance can be... *massaged* with a delicate hand." A faint, knowing smile played on her lips. "Think minor antiquities, forgotten masterworks, items with intriguing, if slightly nebulous, histories."

Aron nodded, already flipping through an art market report. "I've identified a few lesser-known Dutch Golden Age pieces, a couple of early English landscapes, and a surprisingly undervalued collection of pre-Raphaelite sketches. All within a plausible price range for our initial 'acquisitions,' and all with fragmented ownership histories. Perfect for creating a few convenient gaps."

"Gaps we will fill with our own 'discoveries'," Seraphina finished, a glint in her eye. "We'll need to establish a convincing narrative for the collection. Perhaps a recently unearthed private estate, a reclusive connoisseur. Something that explains the sudden appearance of these pieces on the market."

"I've been thinking along those lines," Aron said, tapping the quill pen against his chin. "How about the *'Lost Legacy of the Cavendish Collection'*? A fictional lineage of eccentric aristocrats, their art tucked away for generations, only now coming to light because of unforeseen circumstances... like, say, a distant, previously unknown heir who needs to liquidate assets."

Seraphina clapped her hands together, a rare display of unbridled enthusiasm. "Brilliant, Aron! The Cavendish name has just enough aristocratic ring to it. We'll need to create a believable backstory for this heir – a charming, slightly dishevelled academic, perhaps, who is overwhelmed by the discovery of such a treasure. We'll need a face for that role, someone who can play the part convincingly."

"I have a few contacts in that line of work," Aron mused. "Former theatrical types, always looking for an interesting performance. Someone with just enough genuine enthusiasm for art, and a healthy dose of naivety. It'll make our 'discovery' all the more poignant."

"And the experts," Seraphina continued, her voice dropping to a more serious tone. "The authentication will be the trickiest part. We can't risk actual art historians scrutinising these pieces too closely."

"We shan't," Aron assured her, his voice low. "We'll utilise a network of... consultants. Retired academics, lesser appraisers – men more easily swayed, or simply less particular in their diligence. We shall furnish them with impeccable, though entirely invented, histories for our pieces. Old ledgers, faded correspondence... the sort of detail that whispers authenticity to the unwary eye. Scrutiny, Seraphina, that we simply won't permit."

"Precisely," Seraphina said, her smile returning, a glint in her eye. "We'll orchestrate the entire affair from beginning to end. The pre-exhibition stirs, the exclusive viewing soirees, the carefully worded notices for the gazettes. Every detail must be meticulously arranged to ensure that by the time anyone considers questioning the authenticity, the *'Sleeping Venus'* will have long departed our shores, and our Cavendish heir will have vanished into the mists of the Continent."

A comfortable silence enveloped the pair, with the only sound to be heard being Aron's quill scratching against the paper as he recorded more notes to their developing scheme. As they secured the rooms at Freemasons Hall, the Covent Garden Mirage started to take shape, and they meticulously put each piece of the plan into place. The thrill of the impending game was palpable, and Seraphina felt a familiar surge of anticipation. The planning, after all, was half the fun…

The gas lamps of Covent Garden cast a soft, almost theatrical glow upon the wet cobblestones, painting long, dancing shadows that stretched towards the imposing, neoclassical façade of the Freemasons' Hall. Carriages, gleaming with polished brass and deep lacquered wood, drew up in a continuous, elegant procession, disgorging their cloaked and bejewelled occupants onto the sidewalk.

Inside the grand hall, it now hummed with a genteel excitement, a delicate frisson of anticipation that rippled through the gathered elite of Regency London. Whispers, rustles of silk, and the soft clink of champagne glasses mingled with the faint scent of expensive perfume and pipe tobacco. Everyone turned their eyes and eager faces towards the velvet-draped entrance, waiting for the unveiling of the "curated collection" that had set society abuzz.

Seraphina, in a gown of midnight blue velvet that seemed to absorb the very light around her, moved through the throng with the effortless grace of a swan on still water. Her smile was an art form in itself – warm, inviting, yet with a subtle hint of something unreadable, a promise of hidden depths.

"My dear Lady Seraphina," Lord Ashworth, a portly man whose wealth was only surpassed by his pomposity, boomed, his monocle glinting under the chandeliers. "A most remarkable collection, truly. This 'Cavendish' fellow, quite the enigma, eh? To think such treasures lay hidden for so long!" Seraphina's laughter, light and melodious, tinkled through the air.

"Indeed, Lord Ashworth. Mr Alistair Cavendish is a man of singular pursuits, more at home amidst ancient texts than the glittering salons of London. It has been a considerable task, I assure you, to persuade him to part with these magnificent works." Her gaze drifted, as if in genuine reverence, towards the centrepiece of the exhibition: Dubois's 'Sleeping Venus.'

The painting was breathtaking. Bathed in the soft glow of strategically placed candelabras, the goddess seemed to breathe, her form exquisitely rendered, her slumber peaceful, almost too real.

Around it, the 'Lost Legacy of the Cavendish Collection' glittered – the Dutch landscapes with their impossibly vibrant hues, the English vistas shrouded in a romantic mist, the Pre-Raphaelite sketches, their delicate lines speaking of a nascent artistic movement.

Aron, in a perfectly tailored frock coat, played his part with understated brilliance. As the exhibition's 'curator' he moved discreetly, offering insights, sharing anecdotes about the enigmatic Cavendish lineage, and subtly guiding conversations.

"Notice the brushwork here, Madam Beaumont," he murmured to a bejewelled dowager, gesturing towards a pastoral scene. "The masterful use of impasto, a technique rarely seen with such finesse from this period. A testament to the late Sir Bartholomew Cavendish's discerning eye."

The aforementioned 'Alistair Cavendish' himself was a study in calculated awkwardness. Played to perfection by a former provincial actor named Thomas Finch, he was all nervous smiles and earnest, rambling explanations.

He wore spectacles perched precariously on his nose, his cravat perpetually askew, and spoke with an almost frantic enthusiasm about the "unexpected burden" of his inheritance. He'd gush about the art, then quickly retreat, feigning shyness, making him appealing and, crucially, believable.

"It is truly overwhelming, this... unveiling," Thomas stammered to a group of art enthusiasts, gesturing vaguely at the room. "My great-great-uncle Bartholomew, bless his reclusive soul, truly had a knack for collecting. I confess, I'm more accustomed to... well, to the quiet solitude of research."

Near the entrance, one could hear the subtle hum of the authenticators' voices, their pronouncements carefully choreographed by Aron. These *'experts'* subtly remunerated and presented with meticulously forged documents – the ancient bills of sale, the crumbling correspondence – offered pronouncements of authenticity that solidified the illusion.

"The provenance is impeccable," one would declare, tapping a document with a scholarly air. "A remarkable discovery indeed."

Seraphina drifted towards the 'Sleeping Venus' once more, her heart quickening with a thrill quite unconnected to the artistry itself. The whispers were already circulating: murmurs of staggering bids, of interest from across the Channel, of avid collectors vying for a fragment of this newly unearthed legacy. The very air was thick with covetousness and ambition, a potent draught that Seraphina had so expertly brewed.

The evening's events unfolded successfully, culminating in a triumphant and memorable occasion. With wallets at the ready and reputations poised, London's most distinguished citizens found themselves completely captivated by the prospect of acquiring a Cavendish masterpiece.

As the first bid began, Aron saw the figures flashing across his mental ledger, and Seraphina allowed herself a fleeting, almost imperceptible smile. The Covent Garden Mirage was not merely an exhibition; it was a grand seduction, and London, it seemed, was more than willing to be led.

The Duke of Atherton, known for his discerning eye for portraiture, raised his paddle for the *'Lady of Shalott,'* while across the room, the newly wealthy industrialist, Mr Harrison, aggressively pursued *'The Gilded Cage,'* a rare bird-painting by the celebrated Dutch master, Van der Velde. Even the Countess Lieven, ever the connoisseur of classical sculpture, found herself drawn into a bidding war for *'Apollo's Lyre,'* another piece in the Cavendish collection, against a formidable Prussian envoy. The stage was set, the audience utterly enchanted, and the true performance—the disappearance of the *'Sleeping Venus'*—was drawing closer with every passing, gilded minute.

The scene was prepared for the final, dwindling hour of the exhibition, a moment Seraphina calculated with her usual surgical precision.

It was then, as the last of the aristocratic stragglers lingered, their senses dulled by copious amounts of imported French champagne and the warm, golden glow of self-satisfaction, that the true work would begin.

Seraphina had chosen this precise moment for its peculiar, almost paradoxical blend of heightened visibility and fragmented attention.

Every gentleman present, their guard lowered by the evening's convivial atmosphere, was either deep in earnest, flirtatious conversation with a fair lady, examining a final, intriguing canvas with a feigned connoisseur's eye, or making their reluctant, drawn-out farewells before venturing back into the crisp, chilly London night. It was a perfect, delicate disarray – a stage set for an unseen performance, where the most valuable player would be a ghost among the revellers.

Aron, positioned near a seemingly innocuous velvet rope, gave a subtle nod. Across the room, Thomas Finch, as the bumbling Alistair Cavendish, had escalated his 'nervous' energy. He began to loudly lament the impending sale of "his family's most cherished heirloom," drawing a sympathetic, if somewhat amused, crowd around him. His voice, usually a stammering murmur, now carried across the gallery, a dramatic performance designed to distract.

At that precise moment, a thin, almost imperceptible thread of smoke began to issue forth from a cleverly disguised aperture near the far wall. It was no genuine fire, but merely a harmless, slow-dispersing vapour, cunningly arranged to imitate a minor issue with the warming apparatus within the walls. A faint, rhythmic hum accompanied it, sufficient to catch the ear of a few, but by no means enough to cause a general panic.

"Good heavens, what's that?" someone whispered, pointing.

The few attendants on duty, already tired from the long exhibition, hurried towards the source of the smoke, their eyes scanning for a non-existent fire. Their attention, and that of a few curious onlookers, totally diverted.

This was Seraphina's cue. She moved with almost ghostly swiftness towards the *'Sleeping Venus.'* The painting, secured by heavy chains, was in fact mounted on a specially constructed pivot.

Weeks prior, Aron had bribed an innocent maintenance man to install a series of hidden rollers and a counterweight system behind the wall where the painting hung.

The "chains" were merely decorative, held in place by magnetic clasps. With a precise, almost imperceptible movement, Seraphina located the hidden release mechanism—a tiny, almost invisible button disguised as part of the ornate moulding. She pressed it. A soft click, inaudible amidst the general murmur of the gallery, was her signal.

Behind the wall, in a cramped, dark service corridor, a team of Aron's trusted, silent operatives were already at work. They had entered through a forgotten delivery entrance earlier in the evening, disguised as footmen.

Now, as Seraphina hit the button, the 'Sleeping Venus,' on its specially crafted backing, smoothly pivoted inwards. In a matter of mere seconds, the mechanism able to draw the painting into the service corridor. Working with exceptional precision and coordination, Aron's team functioned like a well-oiled machine as they carefully detached the canvas.

The frame itself, a masterpiece of gilded gesso and carved wood, remained undisturbed—a perfect decoy. A flawlessly executed, high-quality replica of the *'Sleeping Venus,'* painted with remarkable precision by a less scrupulous hand, was already waiting.

This copy, fractionally smaller, intended to nest precisely within the original frame once the true painting was withdrawn, and deftly slipped into place. The chains were re-secured with their ingenious, spring-loaded catches, and the entire assembly pivoted smoothly back into view, appearing exactly as it had moments before. To the casual eye, nothing whatsoever had changed.

As the replica settled, Seraphina allowed herself a fleeting glance at the now "secure" painting. She saw a well-meaning attendee peer closely at it, then nod in satisfaction. The ruse was complete.

Meanwhile, Thomas Finch, seeing Seraphina's signal, suddenly clutched his chest. "Oh, dear! I... I feel quite faint! The excitement... it's too much!" He stumbled dramatically, catching himself on a nearby plinth and narrowly avoiding a priceless porcelain vase. A wave of concern rippled through his small audience, diverting their attention even further.

Aron moved with practiced ease through the throng, his presence barely registering amid the swirl of this charade. As he passed Seraphina, his hand brushed hers—no more than a whisper of contact—and a small, leather-bound ledger slipped from his inner pocket into her gloved hand.

"The deposits are made," he murmured, his voice a quiet current beneath the din of distant laughter. "All accounts have received their funds." The proceeds from the sale of the Cavendish Collection, in your name, now rest securely at Messrs Drummond's on Lombard Street."

Seraphina had been adamant: the funds must be gathered discreetly, transaction by transaction, from collectors lured by the allure of prestige and rarity. Each payment, quietly accepted, became a stitch in the intricate tapestry of her escape. By night's end, the money had vanished into the vaults of a venerable institution—secure, silent, and unreachable by any who might soon awaken to suspicion.

Seraphina gave Aron a nod so slight it could have been mistaken for a blink. "Excellent," she said, her voice cool and composed, as a flicker of triumph danced behind her eyes.

As the haze in the gallery thinned, the attendants reappeared, visibly abashed. "False alarm, ladies and gentlemen," one announced with a strained smile. "Just a faulty flue—nothing to trouble yourselves over."

The crowd murmured with relief, laughter returning like a tide. And as the evening drew to a close, Seraphina and Aron slipped effortlessly into the stream of departing guests. They exchanged cordial farewells with several distinguished figures, their expressions serene, their pace unhurried. In the cloakroom, they paused with quiet precision, collecting their carefully chosen coats and hats—garments selected not merely for warmth, but for the roles they played in the night's quiet vanishing act.

Just beyond the main entrance, Aron had arranged for a private carriage—unmarked, discreet, waiting like a loyal accomplice in the shadows. Inside, the true 'Sleeping Venus' lay hidden: a priceless roll of painted linen, stripped of its ostentatious frame and tucked safely out of sight. The grand facade had been left behind, discarded like a costume no longer needed.

As they stepped into the cool night, the air kissed their skin—a welcome balm after the stifling opulence of the gallery. Seraphina felt the reassuring heft of the ledger in her gloved hand, its weight a quiet declaration of success. Illicit, yes. But exquisite.

The carriage glided through the gaslit veins of Covent Garden, its wheels whispering over cobblestones. It moved like a secret, carrying them away from the glittering, gullible world of the exhibition—where art had been admired, deceivers had mingled, and no one had noticed the masterpiece vanish.

As they rode, Seraphina glanced at Aron, a wicked sparkle in her eyes. His usually sharp, calculating gaze held a quiet, profound satisfaction, and then, a slow, shared grin spread across their faces.

"Another triumph, wouldn't you say, Aron?" she murmured, a genuine, unburdened laugh finally bubbling up from deep within her. The sound was light, almost musical, a stark contrast to the tension of the evening. Aron chuckled, a rich, resonant sound that filled the carriage. "Indeed, my dear Seraphina. A true mirage. And they won't know what hit them until dawn."

As the two dissolved into quiet, mirthful laughter, the sound muffled by the carriage walls, a private celebration of their audacious scam, vanishing into the indifferent London night.

The carriage, having navigated the gaslit warren of Covent Garden's backstreets, drew to a quiet halt before Seraphina's elegant, unassuming home. The very air around it seemed to breathe a sigh of relief, a stark contrast to the glittering deception they had just left behind. As Aron helped Seraphina alight from the carriage, the memory of the night's events became a ghostly echo.

The heavy oak door swung open, revealing the warm, inviting glow of a fire within. Seraphina stepped over the threshold, pulling off her gloves with grace. The scent of roasted pheasant, prepared earlier by her trusted housekeeper, mingled with the earthy aroma of port wine. This was their sanctuary, a quiet haven where the masks of London society could finally be shed.

Aron, carrying a canvas-wrapped bundle that now contained the true *'Sleeping Venus'*, placed it carefully in a discreet, padded chest tucked away in a shadowed alcove. "Safe and sound," he murmured, his voice a low rumble of satisfaction.

Seraphina moved to the decanter, pouring two generous glasses of ruby-red port. The flicker of the firelight danced in her eyes as she handed one to Aron. "To the 'Lost Legacy of the Cavendish Collection'," she toasted, her voice soft, imbued with a deep sense of contentment. Aron clinked his glass against hers. "And to the architects of its 'discovery'," he added, a rare, genuine smile gracing his lips.

They settled into the plush armchairs before the crackling hearth; the warmth seeping into their bones. The tension of the evening dissolves, replaced by a quiet elation. Seraphina leant her head back; her gaze fixed on the dancing flames. "Did you see Lord Ashworth's face when he committed to the *'Dutch Master'?"* she chuckled, a melodic sound that filled the room. "The man truly believes he's acquired a unique piece of history."

Aron laughed softly. "He was practically salivating over it. And pre-Raphaelite sketch you suggested, the one of the fae child? Madam Beaumont declared it had 'unmistakable provenance' from a newly unearthed journal. She'll be boasting about that for weeks."

They spoke for a long while, reliving the moments of the evening, dissecting each nuance of their deception with the precision of seasoned strategists. It wasn't just the thrill of the take; it was the intellectual dance, the anticipation of each step, the subtle manipulation of human desires. They had spun a web of illusion so convincing, so perfectly tailored to the desires of Regency society, that their marks had practically woven themselves into it.

As the hours drifted by, the initial adrenaline of their success mellowed into a comfortable intimacy. The port decanter emptied, and the fire in the hearth dwindled to glowing embers. Seraphina found herself resting her head on Aron's shoulder, a gesture of quiet trust. His arm came around her, a protective, grounding presence.

"Another grand success," Seraphina murmured, her voice laced with a gentle weariness. "What shall we do with ourselves now, Aron? Besides counting our spoils, of course."

Aron stroked her hair, his thoughts already drifting to the next deception. "Perhaps a quiet sojourn on the continent. The art markets of Paris and Rome are always... intriguing. And after all, 'Alistair Cavendish' might just require a change of scenery for a time." He paused, a new spark igniting in his eyes. "Though I daresay, London always seems to call us back, doesn't it?"

Seraphina smiled, a soft, secret smile in the dim light. She knew he was right. The thrill of the chase, the meticulous planning, the exquisite satisfaction of outwitting the unsuspecting – these were the currents that truly animated them. For tonight, however, the silence of their home, the warmth of the fire, and the shared victory were more than enough...

Chapter 3

A Gathering Storm

The morning after their triumph, the Covent Garden air was crisp and clear, a stark contrast to the thick fog of champagne and deception that had clung to the Freemasons' Hall. Seraphina and Aron, refreshed by a few hours' sleep and a hearty breakfast, wasted no time. The 'Sleeping Venus,' now unceremoniously rolled and tucked into a discreet leather tube, was ready for its true journey.

Their destination was a quiet, unassuming townhouse in Mayfair, known only to a select few. Inside, a reclusive but immensely wealthy Dutch merchant, Monsieur Dubois, awaited.

He was a man with a singular passion for art and an even more singular aversion to legitimate auction houses, preferring the shadowy world of private, discreet transactions. He also harboured a deep love for his namesake, the artist Dubois, and had been discreetly searching for years for any of the painter's unlisted works.

"Monsieur Dubois, a pleasure as always," Seraphina purred, her smile as captivating in the sober light of day as it had been under the exhibition's chandeliers. She presented the rolled canvas.

Dubois, a gaunt man with piercing blue eyes, unrolled the painting with trembling hands. His usually impassive face softened as the 'Sleeping Venus' was revealed, her slumbering form catching the light from the tall windows.

He ran a gloved finger along the canvas, his breath held. "Magnifico," he whispered, a rare display of emotion. "More exquisite than I could have imagined. And the provenance... the Cavendish legacy... truly remarkable."

Aron, ever the realist, had already laid out the necessary paperwork – a meticulously forged bill of sale, a fabricated letter from the 'Cavendish heir,' and a carefully worded confidentiality agreement. The price, a staggering sum of twenty thousand guineas, had been agreed upon beforehand, a figure that would solidify their financial independence for years to come.

Within minutes, the transaction was complete, the heavy leather satchels of coin exchanged for the priceless canvas. As they departed, leaving Dubois to marvel at his new acquisition, Seraphina felt a profound sense of closure. The 'Sleeping Venus' had found it's true, if illicit, home...

Thomas Garrick

Meanwhile, across town, within the considerably less opulent confines of the Bow Street Runners' office, the typically placid morning routine was already underway. Thomas Garrick, a principal officer whose quiet manner masked a razor-sharp intellect, found himself increasingly disquieted. He hunched over his desk, a map of London spread before him, punctuated by red crosses marking various noble residences.

"Another one, Mr Garrick," his junior aide, a Watchman, Jack Miller, announced, placing a fresh report on the desk. "The Montrose ball last night. Lady Montrose reports a significant pearl necklace, a family heirloom, missing from her private dressing room."

Garrick sighed, pushing his spectacles up his nose. This was the fifth such incident in as many months. A silver snuffbox from the Fitzwilliam soirée, a diamond brooch from the Ashworth gala, a rare timepiece from the Kensington musicale, and now Lady Montrose's pearls. Each theft had occurred during a grand social event, a ball or a musical, where London's elite gathered to flaunt their wealth and status. Each criminal acted with a perplexing subtlety, leaving no forced entry, no witnesses, only a chilling void where a priceless item once lay.

"Remarkable," Garrick murmured, tracing a path between the marked houses with his finger. "No signs of forced entry. No commotion. And always, it seems, after the appearance of a new face to the social season, or a significant family event." He paused, his gaze fixed on a notice announcing the highly anticipated 'Coming Out' ball for the young Lady Arabella Finch, daughter of a prominent member of Parliament.

"What is the link, Miller?" Garrick mused aloud, his voice barely a whisper. He traced a finger along the map, connecting the crimson crosses with an invisible thread. "This isn't merely opportunistic thievery, a string of isolated incidents. No, this suggests a calculating mind, a highly refined and audacious intelligence at play. Someone with

40

the means to infiltrate these exclusive circles with chilling ease, to blend seamlessly into the gilded tapestry of high society, to observe, to meticulously plan."

He leant back in his creaking wooden chair, the familiar prickle of intrigue, sharp and exhilarating, stirring within him. These weren't the common street ruffians, driven by desperation, or the clumsy housebreakers he typically pursued. This was something far more intricate, more daring, a carefully choreographed larceny that spoke of a different breed of criminal. And as the social season hurtled towards its glittering zenith, with grand balls and opulent soirees planned nightly, a chilling premonition settled over Garrick. The quiet thefts, once almost dismissible, were escalating with an unnerving precision, and he harboured a growing, undeniable suspicion: the individual, or perhaps individuals, responsible were only just beginning their intricate, dangerous dance. The game, he knew, had only just begun.

Lord Ashworth Estate

Thomas Garrick, a man whose quiet methodical nature belied a mind like a steel trap, sat across from Lord Ashworth in the latter's opulent drawing-room. The air, thick with the scent of pipe tobacco and old money, felt heavy with the weight of unease. "Lord Ashworth," uttered Thomas Garrick, "I wonder if I could persuade you to hold a grand ball?" Ashworth, still preening from his acquisition of the *"Dutch*

Master" from the Cavendish exhibition, was initially reluctant to entertain the notion of another grand affair.

"Another ball, Garrick?" Lord Ashworth boomed, adjusting his silk cravat. "My dear Garrick, we just concluded the most splendid exhibition at the Freemasons' Hall! And frankly, the cost of these events is not insignificant. One must consider one's coffers, even amongst society's elite." He gave a dismissive wave of his hand, clearly more concerned with his financial outlay than the string of puzzling thefts.

Garrick, however, remained unperturbed. His gaze was steady, his voice low and calm, yet carrying an undeniable undercurrent of authority. "My Lord, I understand your reservations. However, the thefts are escalating. Lady Montrose's pearls, your own diamond brooch earlier in the season – these are not isolated incidents. We are dealing with an individual, or perhaps a syndicate, of remarkable audacity and skill. They strike only at the most prestigious gatherings, within the most secure residences, leaving scarcely a trace."

He paused, allowing his words to sink in. "Consider the pattern, my Lord. Each item stolen is of immense value, not merely monetary, but often of great sentimental and historical significance. The thief operates with an intimate knowledge of your routines, your homes, and the very fabric of London society." Garrick leant forward, his eyes holding Ashworth's. "I believe the very light and spectacle that a grand ball provides will draw them, and they will use it as a cloak for their designs."

Lord Ashworth scoffed, though a flicker of concern now touched his eyes. "But how would another ball assist you, Sir? Surely, it would merely provide another opportunity for this elusive criminal?"

"Precisely, my Lord," Garrick replied, a hint of a smile playing on his lips. "It would provide an opportunity, yes, but this time, it would be our opportunity. A carefully constructed trap. I require a controlled environment, a setting where we can anticipate their movements, observe their methods, and finally apprehend them."

He produced a small, leather-bound notebook and a pencil. "We would need to work in the utmost secrecy, of course. No hint of our intentions must reach the thief's ears. I propose a seemingly spontaneous event, a grand masked ball perhaps, to create an air of intrigue and to encourage the thief to operate under the guise of anonymity. My men would strategically place themselves, disguised as part of your domestic staff, your musicians, even as guests themselves.

Ashworth's brows furrowed in thought. The idea of outsmarting such a cunning criminal, of being instrumental in their capture, began to appeal to his vanity. And a masked ball… that did sound rather thrilling.

"And what would we use as bait, Garrick?" he inquired, a predatory glint entering his eyes. "What would be enticing enough to draw this fox into our carefully laid snare?"

Garrick paused, his gaze momentarily distant, as if already picturing the scene. "Something of immense value, my Lord, but more importantly, something that embodies the very essence of the collection, these thieves seem to favour. Something with a history, a story, a connection to the very heart of Regency society." He met Ashworth's gaze once more, his voice dropping to a near whisper. "I believe your prized *'Dutch Master'*, recently purchased from the Cavendish Collection, would make for the most tempting centrepiece, wouldn't you agree?"

A flicker of unease crossed Lord Ashworth's aristocratic features. His "Dutch Master"—the undisputed pride of his newly refurbished gallery—to use it as 'bait'? The thought was jarring, almost sacrilegious. Yet, the sheer audacity of the challenge, the potential glory of personally ensnaring this elusive phantom, was a powerful, almost irresistible lure. Slowly, a daring trap began to coalesce in his mind, and Lord Ashworth, despite his initial reluctance, found himself inexorably drawn into Garrick's carefully woven web.

A visitor

The next day, as the crisp morning air held a deceptive innocence, Seraphina, her face carefully veiled and her customary allure cloaked beneath a demure bonnet, directed her hackney carriage towards Lord Ashworth's formidable townhouse. Aron waited discreetly in the carriage, as he usually did on such delicate occasions, a silent, watchful shadow.

This visit wasn't merely a social call; it was a strategic move in Seraphina's elaborate game. She had first encountered Lord Ashworth a year prior, a few months before her inaugural, highly successful 'swindle' on him of the *Dutch Master*. Since then, she had meticulously cultivated this liaison, understanding its potential to offer not only his considerable influence amongst the peerage but also invaluable insights into the labyrinthine workings of London's highest society. Her ultimate prize, often whispered between Ashworth and her during their increasingly intimate evenings, was the Regent's ear—a coveted position that would open doors to schemes far grander than mere art heists.

After Seraphina gracefully removed her outer pelisse, the valet showed her into Ashworth's private study. Lord Ashworth, resplendent in a crimson velvet dressing gown, greeted her with an indulgent smile, entirely unaware of the true, predatory nature of her intentions, or perhaps blissfully unconcerned by it. They took tea, his gaze lingering on her with proprietary pleasure as he spoke of the recent exhibition, his voice laced with unmistakable pride over his new 'Dutch Master.' Seraphina listened, offering just enough praise and admiration—and, crucially, just the right measure of shared, conspiratorial glances—to keep him utterly captivated, drawing him further into her web with every soft-spoken word.

The conversation was flowing as smoothly as the claret in Ashworth's glass when a sharp rap sounded at the study door. Ashworth frowned, clearly annoyed at the interruption. "Enter," he barked.

The door swung open to reveal a man of understated presence, dressed in a sensible dark frock coat. He possessed a keen, intelligent gaze that seemed to miss nothing, and a quiet confidence that belied his unostentatious attire. This was not a typical social caller.

"Mr Garrick," Lord Ashworth announced, a note of resignation in his voice. "What is the meaning of this intrusion; I currently have business with – Lady Seraphina."

Garrick offered a polite, almost imperceptible bow; his eyes, however, lingering on Seraphina for a fraction too long before turning to Ashworth.

"My apologies, my Lord, I wish to speak with you on a matter of some urgency. The conversation we had the other day – I wished to confirm the arrangements for our… mutual endeavour.

Seraphina's finely tuned instincts flared. Mutual endeavour? The phrase hung in the air, a discordant note in the otherwise harmonious symphony of her carefully constructed visit. Her mind raced, sifting through possibilities, analysing Garrick's calm demeanour, the subtle tension in Ashworth's posture. She offered Garrick a cool, polite nod, her expression unreadable, betraying none of the sudden spike of alarm that tightened her nerves.

Garrick, for his part, did not elaborate, merely met her gaze with an unnerving steadiness before turning back to Ashworth. "I trust all is in order for the proposed event, my Lord?" Ashworth, clearly uncomfortable with Garrick's presence, merely grunted. "Yes, yes, Garrick. All is proceeding as discussed. The invitations will be dispatched by midday."

Seraphina, though outwardly serene, felt an icy knot form in her stomach. An event? Invitations? And Ashworth, her pliable, gossiping conduit, was being tight-lipped. This was highly unusual. She was accustomed to hearing every detail of society's conspiracies from Ashworth, yet this "mutual endeavour" was clearly a guarded secret.

"Why, Lord Ashworth," Seraphina purred, her voice a silken thread as she shifted on the settee, letting the hem of her gown playfully skim the air—just enough to hint at a slender ankle. Her gaze never wavered from Garrick, and a challenge sparkled in its depths. "You quite forget your manners. Will you not introduce me to this... gentleman?"

Ashworth, rattled by Seraphina's sudden, carnal charm and eager to regain control of his study, cleared his throat. "Ah yes, Lady Seraphina, forgive me. This is Mr Garrick, a... a particular associate from Bow Street. Garrick, Lady Seraphina." He fixed Garrick with a sharp, almost punitive look. "Now, Garrick, as you can see, I am quite busy at the moment. Speak to Humphrey, my valet. He will supply you with the details?"

Garrick's eyes lingered on Seraphina a heartbeat longer than prudence allowed, drawn by the dangerous lure of her smile and the ripple of mischief in her posture. The air between them crackled with unspoken provocation, and Lord Ashworth's irritation—thinly veiled, almost brittle—hung over the room like a tall, unwelcome shadow.

Garrick, his gaze having flickered down to the sudden, tantalising vision of Seraphina's ankle before snapping back to her face, seemed momentarily thrown. He recovered quickly, but the brief lapse had been noted by Seraphina. "Indeed, my Lord. My apologies for the imposition. I shall take my leave." He bowed stiffly; his eyes meeting Seraphina's for a charged instant before he turned and exited the study.

After Garrick finally departed, the inviting warmth of the study seemed to dissipate, leaving Seraphina with a sudden chill. Her earlier playful manner vanished, replaced by a prickling awareness. What precisely were Ashworth and Garrick conspiring? And to what end? A shiver, not from the cold, but from a delicious, dangerous anticipation, traced its way down her spine. The intricate game, it seemed, was escalating with the unforeseen introduction of a new player, and Seraphina had been granted an enticing glimpse behind the curtain.

Chapter 4

The Masked Ball

The unsettling encounter with Garrick at Lord Ashworth's had left a prickle of unease beneath Seraphina's elegant facade. Back in the discreet comfort of their Covent Garden home, the quiet satisfaction of the 'Sleeping Venus' sale had evaporated, replaced by a growing urgency.

"A 'mutual endeavour' and 'flawless arrangements'," Seraphina murmured, pacing the sitting room, the rustle of her silk gown the only sound. "Ashworth was unusually tight-lipped. That man gossips about the length of a lady's fingernails; for him to be so guarded means Garrick has him well and truly on a leash."

Aron, ever the realist, was already sifting through the society pages of the Morning Post and the London Gazette. "No public announcements of any new ball from Ashworth's estate," he confirmed, his brow furrowed. "Which means it's either a very private affair, or it's not truly about a social gathering."

"It's a trap, Aron," Seraphina declared, her voice a low, resonant hum that barely disturbed the stillness of the grand drawing-room. She stood beside the ornate fireplace. "I feel it in my bones. Garrick, has a meticulous mind and intelligence, is undoubtedly orchestrating some grand scheme. He is laying bait, and he fully intends for the unsuspecting thief to saunter directly into his snare."

Aron leant back in his armchair, a contemplative frown creasing his brow. "But who, pray tell, is this bait intended for?" he mused aloud.

"He suspects a pattern, that much is undeniably clear," Seraphina continued, a faint, knowing smile playing on her lips. "The incessant string of high-society gatherings, the inexplicable disappearance of valuable objects… None of it," she added with a delicate shrug, "has anything to do with us, of course."

"But that description, my dear Seraphina," Aron interrupted, a wry chuckle escaping his lips, "fits at least half of London's 'gilded cage' of aristocracy."

Seraphina admitted, her voice hushed, that Garrick had looked at her with an unsettling, scholarly curiosity rather than crude suspicion. She believed he didn't fully grasp her nature, but sensed something was wrong. Seraphina asserted the encounter was intentional, and Ashworth had carelessly given Garrick a dangerous connection to their world. The silent understanding of their perilous situation permeated the atmosphere.

They spent the rest of the day meticulously piecing together rumours and reports. Aron sent word to his network of street informants – the discreet coachmen, the observant footmen, the ubiquitous flower sellers – to pay particular attention to anything unusual taking place around the mansion of Lord Ashworth.

Seraphina, in turn, subtly pumped her own social contacts, framing her questions as idle curiosity about the season's upcoming events.

The crucial piece of the puzzle arrived that evening, delivered by a scullery maid from Ashworth's kitchens, paid handsomely by one of Aron's contacts. It was a carelessly discarded, partially burned invitation, fished from a bin.

Aron carefully flattened the singed parchment, his voice a low hum as he read, "A masked ball... Held next Friday evening. And... it requests the presence of guests with a particular interest in... 'Exquisite antiquities and recently unearthed treasures'."

Seraphina's eyes widened, a dangerous, thrilling glint sparking within their depths. "Recently unearthed treasures," she repeated, the words dripping with an almost sensuous irony. "And Ashworth's prized 'Dutch Master' will be its centre-piece, no doubt. The very piece he so 'gallantly' attained from our 'Cavendish Collection'." A slow, wicked smile played on her lips.

The sheer brilliance of Garrick's trap unfolded before them—audacious, almost insolent in its clarity—like a deadly bloom opening in slow motion. He wasn't merely investigating; he was weaponizing their own triumphs, their vaunted conquests, turning them into the most enticing lure imaginable. The masked ball would supply anonymity—a glittering cloak for a thief—yet it would also be a space so meticulously surveyed that every breath of movement was measured.

"He'll have his men hidden among the staff, you'll see," Aron purred, tapping the invitation with a knowing fingertip. "A footman here, a maid there—eyes like hawks, ever watchful for anything untoward. Yes," he added, a note of grudging admiration creeping into his voice, "they'll be watching for any approach toward the valuables, waiting for that single misstep to reveal itself."

Seraphina's smile deepened, a spark of delicious anticipation igniting in her eyes. "Oh, this is becoming 'very' interesting, Aron," she purred, her fingers drumming a soft, rhythmic beat on the table. "Garrick believes he's set the stage, but perhaps... perhaps he's merely provided us with the perfect proscenium for our next performance."

As the captivating game between the thief and Garrick, the Bow Street runner, unfolded, the story reached a tantalising new level that promised to deliver further excitement. Seraphina's sitting room was filled with a palpable sense of tension that was noticeably different from what one might expect. As the scent of strategy permeated the room, it mingled with the lingering, subtle aroma of the celebratory port from the previous night.

Seraphina's lips curled into a slow, calculating smile. "He expects us to be drawn to the 'Dutch Master' like moths to a flame," she mused, tracing an imaginary pattern on the velvet tablecloth. "He wants us to steal it, undoubtedly. He'll have eyes on it, hidden behind potted plants, perhaps, or disguised as overly attentive footmen, knowing its origins are now tied to our past deception. He's using our own reputation against us."

The room fell silent, but it was a thinking silence, not one of defeat. A challenging grin spread across Seraphina's face. "Then we shall give him a reason to believe his trap is working, Aron. We shall attend this ball."

Aron, ever the master of logistics, laid out a detailed floor plan of Ashworth House, gained weeks ago from a bribed steward. "Every entrance, every service stairwell, every blind spot. He will primarily focus on the gallery displaying the 'Dutch Master'. That's where he'll concentrate his forces."

"Precisely," Seraphina confirmed, her eyes glittering with mischievous intelligence. "Which means we will not touch the 'Dutch Master'. To steal it would be to fall directly into his snare. Oh no, Thomas Garrick will find that his trap has merely become another stage for our performance. Our target will be far more... subtle."

The game was on, and Seraphina, the master illusionist, was ready for her next act.

Seraphina and Aron have devised an intricate scheme—a ballet of misdirection that signals Garrick's presence while ultimately confounding him. The masked ball serves as the perfect camouflage, anonymity their greatest asset, granting them the freedom to move, observe, and remain unseen. Seraphina would enter first, resplendent in a gown of deep emerald green silk that commands attention, while a delicate mask preserves an air of sultry mystery. At her side, Aron moves like a shadow made flesh—a dashing, masked escort whose quiet strength perfectly complements her radiance. Their very presence, given Ashworth's earlier discomfort, would be Garrick's first satisfying confirmation that his bait had been taken.

"We must behave exactly as the 'thieves' he expects," Seraphina explained, a mischievous glint in her eyes. "We'll circulate the gallery, showing a keen, almost obsessive interest in the 'Dutch Master'. A lingering gaze, a whispered comment, perhaps even a feigned attempt to get closer, only to be politely deterred by a lurking 'footman'." This, she elaborated, would solidify Garrick's belief that they were indeed the culprits; their focus locked onto his bait.

But while Garrick's attention was fixed on his 'Dutch Master' and his imagined thief, Seraphina and Aron were executing their true objectives. They had learned from their informants that the ball was not merely a social event, but also a pre-wedding celebration for a prominent, if slightly eccentric, Duke and his much younger bride, Lady Eleanor.

People knew that Lady Eleanor, in her youthful exuberance, often wore a magnificent diamond and sapphire necklace, a gift from her fiancé, to every grand occasion. It was a stunning piece, yet not valuable enough to warrant intense guarding like the "Dutch Master," and people would dismiss its theft as a common opportunist picking.

"The necklace will be our diversion," Seraphina revealed. "A visible, yet relatively minor, theft that will confirm Garrick's suspicions of a 'masked thief' striking at his event, but without revealing our true cunning. It will keep his investigation firmly on the path of a mere jewel thief, not the orchestrators of grand illusions."

Aron's smile flickered at the corners of his lips. "And how do we lift the necklace without drawing Garrick's swarming eyes upon us?"

Seraphina's thoughts wandered to Lady Eleanor. "My informants say she's fond of dancing," she replied, her voice a purr. "A masked ball invites a certain playful brazenness."

Aron absorbed the idea, the unspoken plan crystallising between them. "I'll claim a spirited set with her—perhaps a lively contra-dance." He pictured the floor: swirls of silk, the glint of masks, bodies weaving in coordinated chaos—the perfect cover for a delicate, carefully timed action. His fingers twitched with anticipation, already mapping the steps amidst the whirl of the crowd.

While Aron captivated Lady Eleanor, Seraphina would orchestrate a fleeting diversion near the orchestra. A sudden, jarring dissonance from a 'broken' instrument, or the splash and clatter of a 'spilt' drink requiring a momentary flurry of white-gloved hands — just enough to draw a few watchful eyes away from the dance floor, for the critical seconds Aron required. The necklace, a shimmering prize, would then be his.

Undoubtable the morning after, Lady Eleanor's distressed cries would echo through Ashworth House. Her diamond and sapphire necklace, a dazzling statement piece; simply gone. Presumably Garrick, upon hearing the news, would nod with grim satisfaction. Another high-society theft, just as he'd predicted. The masked ball, the anonymity — it all pointed to an opportunistic pilferer, a common thief striking under cover of night. Garrick's trap, he'd convince himself, had partially succeeded; he'd forced the culprits to reveal their true nature, even if they'd slipped through his fingers. The "Dutch Master," however, remained secure in the gallery, untouched. He would be left to pursue the phantom of a petty criminal, while Seraphina and Aron, far away, would be toasting their elegant deception, their true identities and their grander scheme, utterly unsuspected. The puppet master outwitted by his own strings.

The air within Ashworth House thrummed with a nervous energy, a palpable undercurrent beneath the veneer of gaiety. Carriages thronged the cobbled drive, disgorging a dazzling array of masked figures, their identities playfully obscured by silk, feathers, and lace. Seraphina, her emerald gown catching the light with every subtle movement, walked beside Aron, both of them cloaked in anonymity, yet acutely aware of every lingering glance. Her mask, adorned with delicate black lace, framed eyes that missed nothing.

"He's here, Garrick's here!" Aron whispered, his voice a low vibration against her ear as they navigated the crowded entrance hall. His gaze flickered towards a group of liveried footmen, standing perhaps a fraction too stiffly, their eyes scanning the arriving guests with an unnatural intensity. Garrick's men, no doubt.

They proceeded directly to the grand gallery, the heart of the masked ball, and the intended focus of Garrick's trap. There, under the glow of countless chandeliers, stood Lord Ashworth's prized 'Dutch Master,' strategically placed on an easel and bathed in almost reverent light. Seraphina allowed her gaze to linger on it, a contrived admiration, then she subtly signalled Aron to make his move towards it.

"A truly magnificent acquisition, Aron," she purred, loud enough for a lurking 'guest' nearby to overhear. "One could spend an age deciphering its depths." Aron nodded solemnly, playing his part. "Indeed, my lady Seraphina. A testament to discerning taste."

They lingered, observing the subtle movements of Garrick's operatives. They noted the 'butler' who spent too long adjusting a curtain near a side door, the 'musician' who kept his back to the orchestra, his eyes sweeping the room, and the 'guest' in the flamboyant peacock mask who seemed to have no interest in conversation, only observation. Garrick was thorough, but Seraphina was more so.

Their true target, Lady Eleanor, flitted through the crowd, a vision in pale blue silk, her youthful exuberance obvious even beneath her delicate silver mask. As expected, the diamond and sapphire necklace glittered at her throat, catching the light with every turn of her head.

The musicians struck up a lively contra-dance, and the dance floor began to fill with a swirling kaleidoscope of masks and colours. This was Aron's moment. He caught Lady Eleanor's eye and, with a confident smile visible even behind his mask, offered his hand.

"My lady, would you do me the honour?" Aron's voice, deep and charming, cut through the music. Lady Eleanor, delighted by the invitation from the dashing stranger, giggled. "Why, certainly, good sir! I do so adore a spirited dance!"

As they joined the dance, the intricate steps of the contra-dance brought them into close proximity with countless other couples. The air grew warm, the laughter louder, the movements more fluid and chaotic. Aron moved with delicate grace, his dark coat a blur as he spun and dipped with Lady Eleanor. His hands, guiding her through the steps, seemed to drift innocently close to the younger woman's neck.

Meanwhile, Seraphina, with a well-timed, almost clumsy stumble near a group of gossiping dowagers, managed to 'accidentally' send a delicate fan clattering to the floor. The commotion drew the attention of one of Garrick's 'guest-operatives' for just a fleeting moment as she bent to retrieve it. A small, momentary breach in vigilance.

It was all Aron needed. In the whirl of a particularly energetic turn, his fingers, strong and precise, brushed against Lady Eleanor's throat. A barely perceptible click, the whisper-thin snap of a clasp, and the cool weight of the necklace was in Aron's palm, expertly tucked into a hidden pocket sewn into the lining of his coat. The movement was so fluid, so integrated into the dance, that Lady Eleanor felt nothing, suspected nothing.

"A truly exhilarating dance, my lady!" Aron exclaimed as the music drew to a close, releasing Lady Eleanor with a polite bow.

"Indeed!" Lady Eleanor panted, her cheeks flushed with exertion and enjoyment. "You dance with such… passion!"

Aron offered a final enigmatic smile, his eyes meeting hers for a fleeting, intense moment before he melted back into the swirling, anonymous crowd. Seraphina, a silent phantom, materialised at his side. They exchanged no words. A potent, shared understanding, taut with triumph and lingering danger, arced between them. Garrick's meticulously laid trap had sprung, yes, but they had danced through its snapping jaws with a breathtaking, arrogant grace, leaving him to chase the ephemeral, mocking shadows of their escape. The tension, though unspoken, thrummed between them, a thrilling testament to their audacious success.

As the masked ball continued its joyful, oblivious charade within, Seraphina and Aron quietly made their exit, blending seamlessly with the stream of departing guests.

The night air was cool and crisp against Seraphina's face as they stepped into the waiting carriage, the diamond and sapphire necklace now a discreet, yet satisfying, weight in Aron's inner pocket.

Garrick would indeed find his prized 'Dutch Master' untouched in the morning, its secure presence a testament to his vigilance. But a lesser, yet equally baffling, theft would undoubtedly await him, a subtle, infuriating whisper of their continued game.

The diamond and sapphire necklace, now a dazzling collection of loose, glittering stones, lay on Seraphina's work table, awaiting it's quiet, discreet journey to a fence. Its monetary value was certainly welcome, a satisfying addition to their already considerable gains.

They had, of course, already secured the perfect contact in Antwerp—a discreet and trustworthy fence known for his ability to liquidate such exquisite items without arousing suspicion. He would ensure the gems found new, legitimate homes, their illicit origins seamlessly erased. But the true worth of this latest acquisition lay not just in the profit; it lay in the delightful chaos it was sure to sow in Garrick's investigation.

With the 'Dutch Master' remaining safely in its gilded frame, the Bow Street runners would be sent scrambling after a phantom jewel thief, completely unaware of the true masterminds who operated on a far grander, more intricate stage...

Seraphina and Aron: The Philanthropic Gambit

"The Queen's patronage, Aron," Seraphina murmured, her gaze distant, fixed on a future beyond mere thievery. "That is the ultimate prize. It provides an unassailable shield, access to information, and a platform for... any venture we choose."

Aron, ever practical, had already begun his inquiries. "Murmurs abound regarding the 'Grand Royal Charitable Concert for the Orphans of London'," he reported, unfolding a carefully procured handbill. "It's to be held at the Pantheon Theatre; a veritable who's who of the Ton will be in attendance. The Queen's own sister, the Duchess of Gloucester, is a key patron." *(The Ton is the glittering, exclusive circle of aristocrats and*

landed gentry at the pinnacle of Regency society. Fashion, fortune, and lineage reign
here, and a single ball can make or break a season.)

Seraphina's eyes gleamed. "Excellent. A charity that tugs at the heartstrings of the aristocracy, patronised by royalty. It's the perfect vehicle. We won't just attend, Aron. We shall be instrumental."

Their plan was audacious in its simplicity: they would become pillars of the community, renowned for their generosity and their 'discerning' taste. They would donate a substantial sum to the orphans' charity, making sure their name, the 'Seraphina and Aron Fund for the Advancement of Benevolence,' was prominently displayed.

"We need a public face for this, a story," Aron mused. "Something to explain our sudden philanthropy after years of discreet operations." Seraphina smiled, a flash of her old Colette Delacroix-taught cunning. "A sudden, unexpected inheritance from a reclusive distant relative," she proposed. "Perhaps a forgotten Cavendish cousin who, in their dying days, wished to atone for a lifetime of avarice by leaving their fortune to 'deserving and well-connected' individuals who would use it for good. We, of course, would be those individuals humbled by the responsibility."

Aron chuckled, adjusting his spectacles. "The very name 'Cavendish' might give Garrick pause, but it would also simply reinforce the idea of a newly wealthy, slightly eccentric couple. It's a beautifully layered deception."

Their next few weeks were a whirlwind of carefully orchestrated public appearances. They attended minor charitable functions, offered their 'expert' opinions on burgeoning art trends (always praising the genuine works, of course), and slowly cultivated a reputation as generous patrons with impeccable taste and even more impeccable social graces. Seraphina charmed the dowagers with her insightful comments on literature, and Aron captivated gentlemen with his nuanced discussions of the political economy.

The invitations to the Grand Royal Charitable Concert soon arrived, not merely as guests, but as significant benefactors. The esteemed patrons included Seraphina and Aron's names at the top of the list.

"The concert itself will be our public anointing," Seraphina declared the night before the event, examining her gown for the evening – a rich, deep purple, signifying both wealth and a subtle regal aspiration. "We will be introduced to the Duchess of Gloucester. A successful interaction there, and our path to the Queen is all but secured."

Aron, polishing his silver-headed cane, gave a rare, genuine smile. "From the shadows of the Rookery to the very heart of the British court. Who would have thought?"

Seraphina met his gaze, her eyes alight with the thrill of the unfolding game. "That, my dear Aron, is the beauty of *The Velvet Deception and the Lady Swindlers*. One must simply know how to play the long game, and to ensure that even one's good deeds serve a greater, more cunning purpose."

The Grand Royal Charitable Concert: A Philanthropic Debut

The Pantheon Theatre, usually alive with the boisterous clamour of masquerades and public assemblies, now glowed with a refined elegance befitting its royal patronage. Rows of gilt chairs filled the grand hall, facing a stage adorned with swathes of rich velvet and a gleaming orchestra. The air, thick with the scent of expensive perfumes and polished wood, buzzed with the hushed murmur of London's elite. Tonight was not about revelry, but about benevolence, and Seraphina, in her deep purple gown, felt a familiar surge of exhilaration. This was a stage grander than any before, and her performance had to be flawless.

She moved through the receiving line beside Aron, his presence a calm anchor amidst the swirling silks and hushed greetings. They offered polite bows, exchanged pleasantries, and accepted compliments on their "generosity." Seraphina's smile was effortless, her eyes reflecting genuine appreciation for the cause, though her mind was calculating every interaction.

Finally, they reached the Duchess of Gloucester, a formidable woman of regal bearing whose presence commanded respect. Her jewels glittered under the theatre's myriad lamps, catching the light as she extended a gloved hand.

"Mr and Mrs Vance," the Duchess announced, her voice surprisingly warm, as a chamberlain introduced them with the name they had carefully chosen for their charitable persona. "Your magnanimous contribution to the Orphan's Fund has been most gratefully received. It is heartening to see such burgeoning compassion among London's newer, discerning patrons."

Seraphina curtsied deeply, her movements fluid and graceful. "Your Grace, the honour is entirely ours. To see the tireless work being done for these innocent souls… it moved us profoundly. We merely wish to do our part." Her voice was soft, earnest, devoid of any artifice.

Aron offered a deferential bow. "Indeed, Your Grace. When we heard of the plight, and particularly your esteemed involvement, we felt compelled to offer what little we could." He made 'little' sound like a king's ransom, subtly reinforcing their wealth.

The Duchess's eyes, shrewd and experienced, held Seraphina's gaze for a moment longer than customary, a flicker of curiosity passing between them. Seraphina met it with unwavering sincerity, a master of feigned humility.

"A truly noble sentiment," the Duchess finally pronounced, a faint smile gracing her lips. "I do hope we shall see more of your commendable spirit in the future, Mr and Mrs Vance. London's charitable causes are ever in need of such... dedicated hearts."

The concert began, a beautiful symphony unfurling its silken strains to wash over the glittering, opulent audience. Seraphina and Aron sat in their privileged seats, strategically chosen for maximum visibility, accepting discreet nods and approving glances as newly acquired peers. They were no longer merely the mysterious, intriguing couple from the masked ball; they were established patrons, their presence a quiet, undeniable statement, actively contributing to the very fabric of this exclusive society.

A deep, abiding satisfaction bloomed within Seraphina, warming her from the tips of her silk-gloved fingers to the elegant coiffure atop her head. They had meticulously planted the first crucial seed of trust, executing with flawless precision the initial step toward securing the Queen's favour. Every hushed whisper, every deferential bow, was a testament to their masterful deception, bringing them ever closer to their ultimate, dazzling goal.

Garrick's Mounting Frustration

Meanwhile, in his sparse office at Bow Street magistrates, Thomas Garrick stared at the crumpled, discarded theatre programme for the

Grand Royal Charitable Concert. His frustration was a tangible presence in the room, thick as the London fog that occasionally rolled in from the Thames.

"Mr and Mrs Vance," he muttered, his finger tracing the names listed among the significant supporters. The new patrons. Their generosity boundless; their social ascension meteoric. It was all too... neat.

His ongoing investigation into the recent thefts, spurred by the snatching of Lady Eleanor's necklace, was hitting dead ends. His operatives had questioned every masked guest at the ball, scrutinised every servant, but the descriptions of the "masked gentleman" were frustratingly vague, melting into the sea of anonymity that a masked ball afforded. The 'Dutch Master' remained untouched, an infuriating symbol of his failed trap.

"No forced entry, sir," Constable Miller repeated for the tenth time, referring to the various grand houses. "No witnesses. It's as if the items simply vanish into thin air. And now this necklace, right under our noses."

Garrick tapped his pen against the programme. "But why the necklace, Miller? Why not the 'Dutch Master' at Ashworth's? My gut tells me this thief, or these thieves, operates with a grander design than mere trinkets. These aren't common thieves."

He picked up the old report from the "Cavendish Collection" exhibition, his eyes falling on the names of the organisers: Seraphina and Aron. Then he looked back at the concert programme: Mr and Mrs Vance. A newly wealthy couple with impeccable taste suddenly appearing on the scene, making significant donations. The timing of their rise, mirroring the baffling string of high-society thefts, prickled at Garrick's intuition.

"Mr and Mrs Vance," he said aloud, a thoughtful glint in his eye. "Find out everything you can about the Vance family, Miller. Their lineage, their sudden fortune, their previous acquaintances. Every single detail." Miller looked surprised. "But, sir, they are patrons of the Duchess. Above reproach."

"Above reproach is precisely where the most cunning individuals often hide, Miller," Garrick retorted, his voice low and firm. "There's a pattern here, a thread connecting these seemingly disparate events. And I have a growing suspicion that our elusive thief, the one who dances through the most secure of rooms, is not a phantom at all, but someone very much in plain sight, pulling the strings of London's finest society." The hunt was indeed far from over, and Garrick felt a cold certainty that the solution lay not in the shadows, but in the most brightly lit corners of the Ton.

Thomas Garrick was a man obsessed, not with catching a common thief, but with unravelling a grander design. The 'Mr and Mrs Vance', who had so swiftly risen through society's ranks, felt like a persistent burr under his saddle. After the bewildering masked ball, where the 'Dutch Master' remained untouched but a valuable necklace vanished, his intuition screamed of a deeper game afoot.

"Miller," Garrick stated the next morning, pouring over old land deeds and shipping manifests, "I want every scrap of information on these two.' Where did they come from? Who are their connections? This sudden, convenient fortune smells as fresh as last year's fish."

Constable Miller, though accustomed to Garrick's unconventional methods, looked dubious. "Sir, the Duchess has vetted them herself. And their solicitor, Mr Finch, vouches for their late cousin's inheritance from a Cavendish offshoot – a reclusive tea merchant in Bristol, apparently. All seems quite proper."

Garrick scoffed. "Proper is merely a mask, Miller. A well-tailored disguise. That 'Cavendish' name again… it rings too true. The exhibition, the sudden wealth, the charitable debut coinciding with a string of impossible thefts. It's too perfectly orchestrated."

Garrick sent his best men to Bristol under the guise of genealogical research to dig into the supposed tea merchant. He instructed his operatives to inconspicuously observe the Vance's' London residence, noting every visitor, every delivery, every unusual occurrence. He even dispatched a discreet inquiry to the Duchess's household, subtly questioning the circumstances of their introduction to 'Mr and Mrs Vance.' Garrick wasn't looking for proof of outright crime, not yet. He was searching for inconsistencies, for the slightest crack in their carefully constructed facade. He felt with a cold certainty that the answers lay not in the common criminal underworld, but in the shimmering, deceptive layers of high society itself.

Seraphina and Aron: Ascending the Social Ladder

While Garrick unleashed his hounds on their carefully fabricated past, Seraphina and Aron meticulously cemented their place within London's elite. The success of the Grand Royal Charitable Concert had been their official coronation into the upper echelons of philanthropy. Invitations now flowed into their Covent Garden home like a steady tide.

"The Duchess mentioned a private viewing of the Queen's new collection of German porcelain next month," Seraphina announced one afternoon, a subtle triumph in her voice. "An intimate affair, only for the most trusted and discerning patrons. We are to be invited."

Aron noted it down. "Excellent. Proximity to the Queen herself is paramount. It allows for observation, for influence, for the seeds of our grandest design to be sown."

Their days became a delicate dance of social appearances and strategic cultivation. Seraphina charmed the wives of powerful lords with her sharp wit and seemingly boundless compassion for the less fortunate.

She discussed the nuances of charitable governance with prominent lords, subtly weaving in suggestions for future endeavours that always seemed to align with the Queen's known interests. Aron, meanwhile, fostered relationships with bankers and influential merchants, not for new schemes, but to bolster their reputation as shrewd, trustworthy investors, capable of managing sizeable sums of money – both legitimate and otherwise.

The Vance's', as they were now known, cultivated an image of quiet affluence. Their home, a tasteful townhouse on the edge of Covent Garden, became a discreet salon. Here, amidst the gleam of polished mahogany and the scent of hothouse flowers, Seraphina and Aron hosted intimate soirees. Carefully selected guests, a mix of minor gentry, rising artists, and influential intellectuals, found themselves drawn to the couple's effortless charm. Exquisite cuisine, prepared by a French chef discreetly poached from a less discerning household, delighted palates, while conversation, skilfully steered by Seraphina's sharp wit and Aron's thoughtful interjections, sparkled with an almost effortless brilliance. Never, however, was there a hint of their past, nor the audacious means by which their considerable wealth had been amassed.

While the "Dutch Master," Garrick's prized red herring, hung untouched in Lord Ashworth's gallery, a monument to his misplaced focus, the true fruits of their audacious "Cavendish Collection" and the modest necklace Lady Eleanor had so carelessly lost, had long since ceased to be mere baubles. The Vance's' had discreetly channelled and laundered through a series of anonymous investments and shrewd land purchases, swelling the Vance's' coffers into a formidable fortune.

"The key now, Aron," Seraphina murmured one evening, her silhouette framed by the window as she gazed at the flickering candlelight below, "is not just to be present, but to be indispensable." She turned, her eyes reflecting the distant glow. "The Queen's ear is not given freely. It must be earned. Through unwavering loyalty, through a shared vision of progress, and through the subtle, irrefutable conviction that we, the Vance's, are the most capable hands to achieve her desires."

Their ultimate ambition transcended mere wealth. It was to influence court policy, to subtly steer the direction of the realm, perhaps even to orchestrate a royal venture so grand, so undeniably beneficial to the Crown, that it would secure their position beyond the reach of any Bow Street Runner, no matter how tenacious.

As Garrick continued to dig, sifting through the dust of their fabricated past, Seraphina and Aron were already building their future – a dazzling, unassailable reality, designed to blind him with its sheer brilliance.

Chapter 5

A Glimmer of Hope

Eliza Beaumont arrived in London like a fragile moth fluttering into a roaring fire. The year was 1816, and the sprawling metropolis, a bewildering beast of cobbled streets and cacophonous cries, swallowed her whole. Barely eighteen, she had fled a dire situation in the countryside – a tyrannical uncle, mounting debts, and a forced marriage looming like a storm cloud. With little more than the clothes on her back and a small, worn satchel, she was adrift, utterly alone amidst the city's indifferent people.

The first few days were a blur of desperation. She haunted the poorer districts, her genteel upbringing providing no shield against the harsh realities of hunger and fear. She sought work, anything, but her delicate hands, more accustomed to embroidery than scrubbing, found no purchase in the gruff kitchens or bustling laundries. Each passing hour chipped away at her fragile hope, replaced by an icy dread that London, for all its promises, was merely a grander, more terrifying cage.

It was on her third day, shivering in a doorway near Fleet Street, rain plastering her thin gown to her skin; then fate, or perhaps a more cunning hand, intervened. A sleek, private carriage drew to a halt nearby, an island of opulent stillness in the chaotic street. From within, a vision emerged – a lady, elegantly cloaked in deep purple velvet, her movements as fluid as melted wax. She held a parasol, not against the rain, but as an extension of her graceful poise. Even in the gloom, her presence radiated an undeniable air of authority and refinement.

Seraphina's gaze, sharp and intelligent, swept over the street, and for a fleeting moment, it settled on Eliza. There was no pity, no judgement, merely an almost imperceptible pause. Then, as Seraphina walked directly towards Eliza, her footsteps silent on the damp cobblestones, she stared at the crumpled mess in the doorway.

"You look lost, child," she said, her voice a warm, melodic murmur, like honeyed wine. It was a voice that commanded attention, yet offered comfort. "And quite soaked through." Eliza, startled, fumbled for words. "I... I beg your pardon, ma'am. I am merely resting."

Seraphina's lips curved into a gentle, sympathetic smile. "Resting from what may I ask? London is a harsh mistress for those without a purpose." Her gaze then softened as she truly looked at Eliza's face, her eyes taking in the faint traces of refinement beneath the grime and despair. "You are not of this place, are you?" Seraphina's voice was a low, comforting murmur. "There is a certain... delicacy about you. Quite refined."

Eliza, desperate for any kindness, nodded, tears pricking at her eyes. "I... I came from the country, ma'am," she stammered, her voice thin with emotion. "Seeking employment. But it is proving most difficult."

Seraphina paused, her gaze lingering, as if making a profound decision. "Employment, you say?" Her smile widened, revealing a hint of dazzling white teeth. "It so happens I am in need of a lady's maid, a companion. Someone of gentle breeding, capable of managing a polite household, and with a keen eye for detail. The work would be light, the hours agreeable, and the remuneration… generous."

Upon hearing this, Eliza's heart leapt. It felt as though a lifeline had been thrown to her from a sinking ship. "Oh, ma'am! Indeed! I would be most grateful for such an opportunity!"

"Then follow me," Seraphina said simply, her voice carrying a quiet authority as she turned towards her waiting carriage. "My name is Mrs Vance, but you may call me Seraphina." And with a quiet, almost imperceptible word to herself, a sly, knowing thought, she added, '*I believe you may be precisely what I am looking for.*'

As Eliza stumbled after her, hope, fragile but potent, surged through her veins. The elegant lady, Seraphina, was her salvation, a beacon in the terrifying streets of London. She had no way of knowing that she was stepping not into a benevolent haven, but into the intricately woven web of Seraphina's life, becoming an unwitting pawn in a game far grander and more perilous than her naïve mind could ever conceive. The innocent moth had found a beautiful, dangerous flame.

Eliza's Unwitting Apprenticeship

Eliza's initial days in Seraphina's elegant Covent Garden home were a dream compared to the nightmare she had escaped. The house, while not ostentatious, hummed with a quiet order and an air of refined taste.

Eliza is given a comfortable, but small, room, provided with fine, though simple, gowns, and introduced to the polite routines of a gentlewoman's companion. Her duties, as Seraphina had described, were indeed light: managing household correspondence, accompanying Seraphina on her morning calls, and ensuring the smooth running of the daily schedule. Aron, Seraphina's quiet yet ever-present associate, was a figure of polite detachment, often away on "business," but always treating Eliza with a reserved respect.

Seraphina herself was everything Eliza had imagined and more. She was kind, patient, and possessed an encyclopaedic knowledge of everything from classical literature to the intricate nuances of court gossip. She took a genuine interest in Eliza's welfare, listening attentively to her concerns and offering gentle, reassuring advice. Eliza, starved for affection and stability, quickly came to adore her patroness, seeing her as a veritable guardian angel. Yet slowly, subtly, Seraphina's benevolence had extra dimensions. It started with seemingly innocuous lessons.

"Eliza, my dear," Seraphina would begin during a quiet afternoon in the drawing-room, "when one wishes to understand a person, one must observe not merely what they say, but how they say it. Notice the shift in their eyes, the nervous twitch of a hand, the subtle hesitation before a grand pronouncement." She would then instruct Eliza to apply this to the guests at her regular social gatherings, ostensibly to ensure their comfort. Eliza, eager to please, absorbed every word.

Next came the art of conversation. "A true lady, Eliza, does not simply speak; she steers. She learns to ask questions that reveal, to guide the topic to areas where her companion is most vulnerable, or most proud. And always, always, to listen more than she speaks." Seraphina would then have Eliza practise these techniques during their outings, turning polite chit-chat into a subtle extraction of information about families, finances, and social standing.

Soon, these lessons expanded into more intricate territory. Seraphina introduced Eliza to the complexities of financial ledgers, not for household accounts, but for tracking distant, fictitious investments. She taught Eliza how to forge a passable signature, explaining it away as a necessary skill for a companion dealing with proxy documents. She even tutored Eliza in the subtle art of pick-pocketing, disguised as "exercises in hand dexterity" necessary for manipulating delicate fabrics or retrieving dropped items in a crowded ballroom. Eliza, too innocent to question the true purpose, saw it only as another facet of Seraphina's boundless knowledge, another skill to acquire in her journey to becoming an indispensable companion.

"You have a remarkable talent for observation, Eliza," Seraphina would praise, her eyes glinting with a satisfaction that Eliza attributed to pride in her pupil. "And a naturally guileless countenance. These are invaluable assets in society."

Eliza blossomed under Seraphina's tutelage, her natural intelligence awakening. The meek, lost country girl transformed, gaining confidence, polish, and a formidable, albeit unwitting, set of skills in manipulation and subterfuge. She saw herself as growing into the accomplished companion Seraphina desired, unaware that every lesson, every piece of advice, was a carefully laid brick in the foundation of her future as an unwitting accomplice, trained in the art of deception. The seemingly legitimate employment was merely the first silken thread in a web that was slowly, meticulously being spun around her.

Eliza's First Taste of Deception

The day arrived when Eliza, unknowingly, became a vital thread in Seraphina's meticulously woven tapestry of deception. It began, as many subtle deceptions do, with an air of perfect innocence. Seraphina held a delicate, cream-coloured letter, its script wavering with age and a certain aristocratic tremor. It was from elderly, notoriously forgetful Baroness Charlotte – a woman as renowned for her sprawling collection of antique lace as she was for her penchant for misplacing valuable items. The Baroness, in her characteristic muddled fashion, was searching for a particularly rare piece of Venetian point lace, one she vaguely recalled lending to a distant relative years ago. Knowing Seraphina's reputation for a "discerning eye," she had penned a plea for help in its recovery.

"Eliza, my dear," Seraphina began, her voice a soft murmur, as she placed the letter on a polished side table. "The Baroness is quite distressed. She believes someone may have accidentally placed her beloved lace for sale at the next estate auction." Seraphina paused, a sigh escaping her lips. "It would be an act of immense kindness if you could accompany me to the auction house. Merely to observe, of course. Your keen eye for detail, a quality I have often admired in you, would be quite invaluable in discerning such a delicate piece amidst a sea of textiles."

Eliza, flattered by the trust placed in her, readily agreed. The auction house was a bustling, chaotic scene, filled with eager bidders and a cacophony of voices. Seraphina moved through the crowd with effortless grace, engaging in polite conversation, while Eliza, as instructed, discreetly observed the proceedings.

The 'Venetian point lace' was indeed listed, a delicate, stunning piece of work. As the bidding commenced, Seraphina subtly positioned herself near a rather pompous gentleman known for his competitive nature and his aversion to being outbid.

"Such exquisite work," Seraphina murmured to Eliza, just loud enough for the gentleman to overhear. "Shame it's likely a modern imitation. The true Venetian point from that period has a unique, almost invisible, stitch. Only a truly expert eye could discern it."

Eliza, remembering Seraphina's lessons on observation, nodded earnestly. "Indeed, ma'am. The genuine article is quite distinct."

The gentleman, his ego pricked, immediately bid more aggressively, determined to prove his "expert eye." Aron was positioned across the room pretending to be a casual observer, and Seraphina gave him a subtle signal. Aron, exhibiting a carefree air, initiated bidding against the gentleman, thereby causing the price to rise to unprecedented levels.

As the bidding reached an exorbitant sum, Seraphina caught Eliza's eye, a fleeting, almost imperceptible wink. Then, with a sigh of feigned regret, she withdrew from the bidding. The pompous gentleman, triumphant, secured the 'rare' lace at a wildly inflated price.

Seraphina explained later, back at the house, "The Baroness simply wanted to know if her lace had been sold and for what price." We have provided her with that information, and ensured she knows it was a 'genuine' piece, albeit one that fetched a rather remarkable sum." She handed Eliza a small, exquisitely crafted brooch. "For your invaluable assistance, my dear. Your observations were quite precise."

Eliza, beaming with pride, accepted the gift. Unbeknownst to her, the lace the Baroness had mentioned was never even present at the auction, that the item sold was an artful fake, and that her own unwitting comments had only contributed to bolstering the credibility of Seraphina's calculated manipulation of its worth. Performing her role impeccably, she was a pawn in a game she did not yet comprehend, beginning her journey to become a lady swindler in Seraphina's deceptive world.

Garrick's Tightening Net

While Eliza was unknowingly honing her skills, Thomas Garrick's investigation into 'Mr and Mrs Vance' was beginning to yield unsettling results. His men in Bristol had found no trace of a reclusive tea merchant named Cavendish with a fortune to bequeath. The records were either non-existent or suspiciously vague. The solicitor, Mr Finch, who vouched for their inheritance, was a man with a reputation for being overly discreet, and a known associate of less-than-reputable individuals.

"A phantom inheritance, Miller," Garrick declared, slamming a sheaf of papers onto his desk. "And a solicitor who conveniently 'lost' the precise details of the will. This 'Cavendish' story is a fabrication, a flimsy veil, over something far more substantial."

His operatives observing the Vance' residence had also reported peculiar findings. Although their social calendar showed legitimate engagements, odd discrepancies existed. Unmarked carriages arriving at unusual hours. Aron's frequent, unannounced absences. And Seraphina's peculiar habit of receiving discreet, veiled visitors who never seemed to stay long, yet left a distinct air of clandestine business.

Garrick thought hard about how things were related. The 'Cavendish Collection' exhibition, the sudden influx of wealth, the masked ball theft, and this fabricated inheritance. It all pointed to a single, audacious pair. The pieces of the puzzle were beginning to fit, forming a picture of cunning and ruthless efficiency.

"I believe our 'Mr and Mrs Vance' are our elusive thieves, Miller," Garrick stated, his voice quiet but firm. "They are not merely stealing; they are building an empire of deception. They use their ill-gotten gains to buy respectability, to ascend the social ladder, to hide in plain sight."

He picked up a recent society column, featuring a glowing report on 'Mr and Mrs Vance's' latest charitable donation. "They are becoming too powerful, too well-connected. If they gain the Queen's ear, they will be untouchable."

"What is our next move, sir?" Miller asked, a rare note of apprehension in his voice.

Garrick's eyes, sharp and unwavering, fixed on the map of London. "We watch them. Every move. Every contact. We find the true source of their wealth, the real names behind the 'Vance'. And we wait for them to make a mistake. Because even the most cunning of spiders eventually trips on its own web."

The hunt was no longer about recovering stolen jewels; it was about exposing a grand deception that threatened the very integrity of London's highest society...

Eliza's Deepening Immersion

Eliza's days now revolved around a curious blend of genteel domesticity and increasingly intricate lessons in observation and artifice. Seraphina, with her gentle smile and keen intellect, continued to be a benevolent mentor, seamlessly weaving lessons into their daily routines. Eliza, eager to prove her worth and deeply grateful for her escape from destitution, absorbed every instruction like a sponge.

The "exercises in hand dexterity" developed. What began as retrieving dropped items became the nuanced art of manipulating small objects unseen. Seraphina would scatter coins or tiny brooches on a crowded table during one of their calls and challenge Eliza to retrieve them without attracting notice. "A true lady's touch," Seraphina would explain, "is so light it is imperceptible. Eliza's clumsy fingers refined over time, eventually reaching a level of precision that made them suitable for sophisticated and complex tasks.

Conversations became a subtle game of extraction. Seraphina would introduce Eliza to acquaintances, then later prompt her: "Did you notice the Lady Farnsworth's dismissive gesture when her husband mentioned his investments in the East India Company? What might that signify, Eliza?" Eliza, encouraged to share her insights, grew sharper, learning to read the unspoken language of the ton – the subtle shifts in posture, the nervous cough, the guarded glance. She began to see society not just as a collection of people, but as a complex web of vulnerabilities and hidden desires.

Beyond social interactions, Seraphina introduced Eliza to the quiet world of documents. She taught Eliza how to read and write, how to recognise different paper qualities, and even how to create convincing "aged" effects on modern parchment using tea stains and careful creasing. This skill was deemed necessary for managing Seraphina's extensive (and entirely fictitious) family archives. Eliza spent hours meticulously copying old letters, forging dates, and mastering different pen strokes, believing she was merely perfecting her clerical abilities.

One afternoon, Seraphina brought out a selection of valuable, yet subtly flawed, gemstones. "Sometimes, Eliza," Seraphina explained, holding a cloudy diamond to the light, "a thing's true worth lies not in its initial appearance, but in how it is presented. A clever setting, the right light, an interesting story... these can elevate the ordinary to the extraordinary, and disguise the flawed as flawless. Eliza learned to identify subtle imperfections, but more importantly, to understand how to cleverly mask or even use them to enhance a fabricated narrative.

Eliza's transformation was remarkable. The timid country girl was rapidly developing into a poised, observant young woman, fluent in the nuances of high society, and unwittingly mastering the very skills required for sophisticated deception. She felt a growing confidence, a sense of purpose she had never known. She was Seraphina's invaluable companion, and she would do anything to remain in her esteemed patroness's good graces, entirely oblivious to the fact that every lesson was forging her into a vital, unsuspecting piece of Seraphina's world of cunning and deception.

Echoes from Paris

The morning began like any other, cloaked in the deceptive calm that always followed a successful, if minor, deception. Eliza, her brow furrowed in concentration, was meticulously cataloguing Seraphina's extensive collection of rare botanical prints, a task chosen specifically to further hone her already sharp eye for detail. Aron was, as usual, out, discreetly tending to the quiet disposal of a recently acquired necklace and its newly individualised, glittering stones. Seraphina herself sat at her writing desk, the scratching of her quill the only sound, composing a polite, yet subtly influential, letter to a duchess concerning a proposed, and rather strategic, enhancement to the Royal Horticultural Society. The ink flowed smoothly, her thoughts precise and perfectly ordered, her world a meticulously constructed tableau of control.

Then, a small, unassuming package arrived. It had been left by a nondescript delivery boy, no address, no return sender, just a crisp brown paper wrapping tied with plain twine. Seraphina opened it with caution, her instincts prickling. Inside, nestled on a bed of tissue paper, was a single, perfectly preserved white gardenia.

The delicate blossom itself held no threat, but tucked beneath its waxy petals was a folded slip of the finest, almost translucent, vellum. Seraphina's elegant fingers unfurled it. There was no writing, no explicit message. Instead, etched with exquisite precision into the very fibres of the paper, was a tiny, almost invisible Parisian fleur-de-lis, subtly distorted, its upper points subtly bent inwards, like a wilting crown.

A chill colder than any London fog snaked down Seraphina's spine. The quill clattered from her fingers, leaving a dark blotch on the pristine letter. The gardenia, so beautiful moments before, suddenly seemed to exude a faint, cloying scent of memory. This wasn't merely a message; it was a signature. A signature she knew intimately, one that belonged to a ghost she had long believed laid to rest. *Madame Colette Delacroix.*

Flashback: Paris, 1809

The Parisian air, thick with the scent of burgeoning revolution and fading aristocracy, crackled around Seraphina like static. The opulence of Colette's new salon, a stark contrast to the growing unrest outside, was a dazzling, dangerous world of whispered secrets and glittering jewels. Colette Delacroix, a woman of formidable intellect and chilling grace, was more than just a mentor; she was a force of nature. She had refined Seraphina's natural wit into a weapon, sharpening her observations, perfecting her charm, and instilling in her the ruthless understanding that society's elite were merely ripe for the plucking.

Their grandest scheme yet involved the theft of a priceless sapphire from a duke's private collection. The plan was intricate, a masterpiece of misdirection involving forged invitations, disguised identities, and a cleverly constructed 'accident' to create chaos. Seraphina, then known as 'Sylvie,' was Céleste's chosen instrument, poised to execute the final, critical step.

But Colette had an undercurrent of ruthlessness that even Seraphina, hardened by the Rookery, found unsettling. During the execution of the sapphire heist, an innocent chambermaid accidentally discovered a key piece of their deception. Seraphina, following Colette's earlier chilling instructions, was to ensure no witnesses. Yet, as she looked into the maid's terrified, wide eyes, a flicker of humanity, a remnant of the lost girl from St. Giles, rebelled. She created a diversion, allowing the maid to escape, believing herself merely confused by the commotion. They secured the sapphire; the deception was flawless, and the duke remained unaware.

Seraphina returned to Colette, exhilarated by the success, yet haunted by her split-second deviation. Colette, however, possessed an uncanny sixth sense for betrayal. Her eyes, usually cold and calculating, turned to chips of ice. *"You let her go, Sylvie,"* she said, her voice devoid of emotion, more terrifying than any shout. "A loose thread unravels the finest tapestry. Humanity is a weakness, my dear. One that will get you caught, or worse, buried."

The air in the dimly lit salon crackled, thick with unspoken accusations. Colette's eyes, usually sharp with calculating amusement, narrowed into glacial slits, fixed on Seraphina. Seraphina had dared to show a flicker of hesitation, a shadow of conscience, and in Colette's world, such weaknesses were not merely undesirable — they were existential threats.

"A liability," Colette hissed, the word a venomous dart aimed precisely at the chink in Seraphina's newfound armour. The elegant veneer of their partnership fractured, revealing the raw, brutal core beneath. Seraphina, caught between the crushing weight of Colette's wrath and the insistent, surging tide of her own burgeoning independence, fought. It was not a duel of wits, but a desperate, physical struggle, an untamed dance of survival amidst overturned furniture and shattered porcelain. When it ended, Seraphina stood, breathless, her body unmarked, yet her spirit bore wounds far deeper than any blade could inflict. The bond forged in the crucible of shared desperation and ambition lay shattered, its remnants sharp and dangerous.

From that night forward, their interactions became a brittle dance around a chasm of unspoken grievances. Every glance was a judgement, every word a veiled accusation. The tension was a suffocating shroud until; one moonless night, Seraphina slipped away with Colette's treasure chest, a ghost in the pre-dawn quiet. She left no note, no farewell, only the profound hope that the paths of Sylvie and Madam Colette Delacroix would never intersect again…

The gardenia's scent now crowded Seraphina's study, oppressive and impossible to ignore. The bent fleur-de-lis—Collette's familiar, almost brazen signature—was unmistakable. Somehow, she had found Seraphina again.

An icy dread tangled with a fierce, gnawing worry inside Seraphina. Collette was never one to send idle greetings. This was more than a message: a warning, perhaps an invitation into a new, far more dangerous game. The mentor had resurfaced, and the student knew, with a tremor of fear, that the echoes from the past had become a real, immediate threat—destitution and peril closing in as surely as night.

Chapter 6

Garrick Tightens the Net

Thomas Garrick felt the familiar prickle of a predator closing in on its elusive prey. The gardenia sent to Seraphina was a puzzle piece he didn't yet possess, but his investigation into 'Mr and Mrs Vance' was already yielding unsettling connections.

The 'phantom inheritance' from the supposed Bristol tea merchant had dissolved into thin air. His discreet inquiries to the Duchess's household revealed Seraphina's charming, yet curiously vague, account of her newfound fortune.

"Miller," Garrick stated, pointing to a sprawling corkboard adorned with strings and tacked notes, "connect the dots for me. Not just the stolen objects, but the events surrounding them."

Constable Miller, though still prone to Garrick's unexpected leaps of logic, spoke about the patterns they had unearthed: The Fitzwilliam Soirée: A diamond brooch vanished. The host, Lord Fitzwilliam, had just made a significant public investment in a new, unproven shipping venture.

The Ashworth Gala (and the 'Dutch Master' acquisition): The Ashworth family diamond brooch disappeared. Shortly after, Lord Ashworth loudly proclaimed his acquisition of the "Dutch Master" from the 'Cavendish Collection.'

The Kensington Musicale: A rare timepiece went missing. The host, the Earl of Kensington, had recently funded a controversial new opera production that faced financial difficulties.

Lady Montrose's Ball: Her pearls vanished. Lady Montrose was a key figure in a private consortium aiming to develop new lands in the West Indies.

The Masked Ball: Lady Eleanor's diamond and sapphire necklace was stolen. Garrick set a trap for the art thief at the Ashworth Masked Ball, where the 'Cavendish'-linked 'Dutch Master' was prominently displayed; the theft of Lady Eleanor's necklace occurred during this very event.

Then there was the Grand Royal Charitable Concert: No theft reported, but 'Mr and Mrs Vance' made their grand charitable debut, solidifying their high-society standing.

"It's not just about the stolen items," Garrick mused, tapping a finger on a map of London where he had marked the incidents. "It's about the context. Each theft occurs during a significant financial or social manoeuvre by the victim. Lord Fitzwilliam's shipping, Lord Ashworth's art acquisition, the Earl of Kensington's opera, Lady Montrose's pearls disappearing. These aren't random pilfering. They're... reconnaissance, or perhaps, diversions." Miller's eyes widened. "Diversions, sir? But what for?"

"To keep our attention on the minor prize," Garrick explained, his voice low and intense. "To make us chase the glitter, while they play a much larger game. The 'Cavendish Collection' itself, the sudden appearance of masterpieces... it was too perfect. And the 'Vance's' with their fabricated past, their strategic patronage, and their seemingly boundless access to the very heart of society. It's all connected, Miller. A web of high-society swindles designed to manipulate not just wealth, but influence."

He paced his small office, the pieces of the puzzle beginning to click into place with terrifying clarity. "Our thieves aren't merely taking; they are gaining. They're not after trinkets; they're after power, position, and the ability to operate above the law, shrouded by their carefully constructed respectability. The masked ball wasn't a failed trap, Miller; it was a demonstration. A taunt. They wanted us to know they were there, and that they could dance through our finest efforts."

Garrick stopped; his gaze fixed on the name 'Seraphina' from an old exhibition catalogue. "They are remarkably clever, audacious, and utterly ruthless. And they are using London society itself as their primary tool. We must move with extreme caution. We cannot afford to make a single misstep, for if they discover our true suspicions, they will vanish, or worse, turn their considerable talents against us."

Whispers of a Phantom

Thomas Garrick knew the time for passive observation was over. The 'Vance's' were too deeply entrenched, too adept at their game. To expose them, he needed direct testimony, the subtle inconsistencies that would betray their cunning. His chosen method: a series of discreet, seemingly innocuous interviews with the victims and witnesses, aiming to prick at the edges of their gilded memories.

He began with Lord Ashworth, hoping to exploit the nobleman's pomposity and his unwitting connection to Seraphina Vance.

Arriving at Lord Ashworth's estate, Garrick was admitted into a study where a red-faced Lord blustered about the room. Still smarting from the humiliation of the necklace theft of Lady Eleanore, Ashworth clung to the hollow triumph of his "Dutch Master" remaining untouched, unaware of how precarious his position had become.

Garrick listened patiently as Lord Ashworth huffed, "What more can I tell you? The masked rogue vanished like smoke, and Lady Eleanore is still quite distressed!" He gestured toward his new acquisition, which seemed to mock Garrick with its very presence.

Steering the conversation, Garrick asked, "My Lord, let's revisit the 'Cavendish Collection' exhibition. Do you recall meeting the organisers, Seraphina and Aron Vance, there?"

A slight frown creased Ashworth's brow. "Ah yes," he mused, distracted. "Seraphina Vance—she's quite something, you know.

Remarkable woman, quite captivating. And that Mr Cavendish - Rather flustered fellow, but clearly a genuine academic." And yes, I've known Seraphina, Mrs Vance, for several months now. She's a delight to entertain."

"Indeed," Garrick nodded, his voice even. "And the details of the Cavendish collection's provenance? The lost legacy, the reclusive cousin? Did anything strike you as... unusual?"

Ashworth puffed out his chest. "Unusual? Nonsense! The documents were impeccable! Old bills of sale, letters... all handled by Mr Finch, a most discreet solicitor, I might add. He provided all the necessary assurances."

Garrick paused, then gently probed. "And your impressions of Mrs Vance, Seraphina Vance herself? Did her manner, her knowledge of art, seem... unexpectedly profound for someone merely introducing a collection?" He watched Ashworth closely, knowing the man's weakness for beautiful, intelligent women.

Ashworth chuckled, a lecherous glint in his eye. "Profound? My dear Inspector, she was utterly enchanting! Her insights into art were quite delightful for a lady. But no, nothing 'unexpected. Merely a woman of refined taste and good breeding. Quite the catch, if only she were mine." Garrick made a note. Ashworth, blinded by charm, offered no real insights.

Next, Garrick called upon Lady Eleanor, the unfortunate victim of the necklace theft. Still visibly agitated, she was nonetheless eager to recount her ordeal. "As I remember," she began, fluttering her fan with a dramatic flourish, "I was asked to dance by a masked gentleman! He danced with such grace, such passion! And his hands... so strong, yet so gentle. I felt nothing, truly nothing, until later when I discovered my necklace was gone!"

"Did anything about him seem... out of place, my lady?" Garrick pressed, his voice even. "His accent, his mannerisms, his eyes behind the mask? Anything at all that might distinguish him?"

Lady Eleanor searched her brain; her brow furrowed in concentration. "No, not at all!" she exclaimed, shaking her head. "He moved like one of us. So polite, so charming. Perhaps a little too charming, now that I think of it, for someone whose name I never quite caught. He simply said he admired my spirit." She sighed; a wistful expression crossing her face. "He was utterly unremarkable in the most remarkable way."

Garrick's gaze drifted to the framed portrait of Lady Eleanor's fiancé, the duke. He had been present at the ball, yet strangely oblivious to the subtle drama unfolding on the dance floor. "And the music, my lady? Any disruptions during your dance?"

"Only a slight disruption, I recall," Lady Eleanore mused. "A musician bumped into someone near the pit and dropped some sheet music. A trifle, really, barely noticed amidst the waltz."

Garrick's jaw tightened. A "trifle," a "barely noticed" moment. He was certain that this seemingly innocuous event was linked. The pieces of the puzzle were there, but maddeningly out of reach.

He could feel the cold precision of the thieves' minds at work. He knew he was questioning players in a game the criminals still controlled, their performance so perfect, their deception so seamless, that even the victims couldn't see past the velvet illusion. The whispers of a phantom thief were growing louder, but the faces behind the masks remained stubbornly out of reach.

A Perilous Tea

The invitation to Lady Montrose's afternoon tea arrived with all the delicate formalities befitting a close friend of the Duchess of Gloucester. For Seraphina and Eliza, it was another carefully placed stepping stone towards the Queen's inner circle. Lady Montrose, a well-connected widow with a penchant for charitable causes, had become a recent, enthusiastic admirer of Seraphina's philanthropic zeal. Eliza, now increasingly poised and observant, was blossoming in her role as Seraphina's constant companion, completely unaware of the intricate currents flowing beneath the surface of their new life.

The Montrose drawing-room, bathed in the soft glow of an early afternoon sun filtering through tall windows, was a symphony of pastels and polite chatter. Porcelain teacups clinked, silver teapots gleamed, and the air hummed with the gentle murmur of society's elite exchanging pleasantries and covert gossip. Seraphina, in a gown of elegant dove grey, moved with effortless grace, engaging Lady Montrose in a discussion about the merits of a new orphan refuge, her voice a soothing balm of refined concern. Eliza, sitting attentively nearby, observed the room with her newly sharpened gaze, noting the intricate lace on a dowager's cap, the subtle tension in a young man's jaw.

Then, across the room, near the large French windows overlooking the manicured gardens, Seraphina's smile faltered. Her heart, usually a steady, unwavering drum, skipped a beat, sending a cold jolt through her veins. Standing in animated conversation with a group of elderly gentlemen were two figures she never wished to see, certainly not together, and certainly not here.

The first, unmistakable in his quiet intensity, was Thomas Garrick. He was listening intently, his sharp eyes, even from a distance, seeming to absorb every detail of his surroundings. Seraphina felt a familiar prickle of recognition – the same unnerving steadiness she'd observed in Lord Ashworth's study. His presence here at a private afternoon tea was highly irregular for a Bow Street Runner, confirming her fears that his investigation was intensifying beyond mere theft.

But it was the second figure that truly sent a chill of visceral dread through her. A woman Seraphina would never forget stood beside Garrick, her back to Seraphina. The elegant sweep of her dark hair, styled in a severe, yet undeniably fashionable French pleat, the imperious tilt of her head, the way her hand, adorned with a single, striking emerald ring, gestured with subtle authority. It was Madame Collette Delacroix.

The gardenia, still subtly perfuming Seraphina's study back home, had been a prelude. Now, Colette was here, in the flesh, not just a whisper from her past, but a tangible, terrifying presence. She looked older, with a hint of weariness around her piercing eyes, but no less formidable. And the fact that she was conversing, seemingly at ease, with Garrick, the very man hunting Seraphina, twisted the knife deeper.

A wave of fragmented memories, sharp as broken glass, flashed through Seraphina's mind: the scent of her old home, the glint of Colette's eyes just before Seraphina made her escape. She forced herself to breathe, to keep her composure, to maintain the serene façade of Mrs Vance.

Eliza, noticing the sudden, almost imperceptible stiffening of Seraphina's posture, leant in. "Is something amiss, ma'am?" She whispered, her brow furrowed with concern.

Seraphina managed to regain her smile, though it felt brittle, stretched. "No, my dear," she replied, her voice steady, a testament to years of training in deception. "Merely a passing chill. I believe I saw an old acquaintance from my younger days. Quite unexpected."

Unexpected was an understatement. The presence of Colette, and her proximity to Garrick, signified a confluence of threats Seraphina had never anticipated. The game had just shifted dramatically and perilously, and Seraphina knew, with a certainty that turned her blood to ice, that she was now caught between two formidable forces, each capable of utterly destroying her carefully constructed world...

A Game of Cat and Phantom

The Montrose drawing-room, once a haven of polite conversation, had become a minefield for Seraphina. Her eyes, hidden behind a veneer of serene interest, never strayed far from the formidable pairing of Thomas Garrick and Madame Colette Delacroix. Colette, draped in an exquisite gown that spoke of French haute couture rather than London fashion, captivated a small circle of guests with anecdotes that were just plausible enough to entertain, yet subtle enough to steer conversations away from anything truly revealing. She was playing a game, Seraphina realised, a master manipulator at work, weaving a spell over the very man tasked with unravelling London's illicit underworld.

"And so, my dear Mr Garrick," Colette purred, her voice carrying a faint, exotic lilt, "one hears whispers of these masked thieves. Quite a scandalous affair! Do you find the London underworld as… challenging as our own Parisian rogues?" She flashed Garrick a knowing smile that suggested shared, clandestine understanding.

Garrick, though clearly exasperated by his superiors' demands for an arrest, merely offered a curt, professional nod. He looked utterly worn, burdened by the pressure his own boss was exerting. Seraphina caught his eye across the room; his gaze was direct, solid, but there was a flicker of something new – a simmering frustration, a desire for any tangible lead. He gave a slight, almost imperceptible shake of his head as if to say, this is going nowhere.

Lady Montrose, beaming with pleasure, made her way towards Seraphina. "My dear Mrs Vance," she announced, drawing Seraphina gently towards the group, "you simply must meet Madame Delacroix'. She has just arrived from Paris and possesses the most fascinating insights into Continental society."

Seraphina's heart pounded a frantic rhythm against her ribs. This was the moment. She offered her most polished smile, her eyes sparkling with feigned delight. "Madame Delacroix, good day to you."

Collette turned, her gaze sweeping over Seraphina with a casual, almost dismissive air. "Madame," she acknowledged, a cool politeness in her tone. Her eyes, so sharp, seemed to pass over Seraphina's features, recognising the elegance, the breeding, but not the girl she had taken from the gutter. Not her Sylvie. Seraphina held her breath, becoming merely Mrs Vance—the compassionate philanthropist, a woman of refined taste; revealing not a trace of her former self, the Rookery or the London underworld. But Colette's cold, appraising glance lingered, then slid away. Seraphina exhaled, surprised at how steady she remained. Her new persona proved impenetrable.

As the conversation continued with the group for a short while, Seraphina would answer with polite and noncommittal responses. In contrast, Garrick's demeanour shifted, and he became visibly uneasy. Having run out of patience, he then proceeded to offer his excuses. But as he was leaving, he brushed past Seraphina; their eyes met for a fraction, and the look he cast—sharp, calculating—held a challenge. "Mrs Vance," Garrick said, his voice dropping to a low, almost intimate tone, audible only to her amidst the polite murmur of the drawing-room. "This has been most… illuminating. I would find it most helpful to call upon you soon to discuss a matter of significant public interest. Perhaps tomorrow?"

It wasn't a request; it was a veiled summons. Garrick, too, was playing a game, subtly turning his frustration into a direct approach, hoping to catch her off guard. Seraphina's polite smile didn't waver. "Of course, dear Mr Garrick. My door is always open to a gentleman of such dedication. Do call."

Garrick gave a curt nod and swiftly exited the drawing-room, leaving the clatter of teacups behind. Seraphina felt a strange mix of relief and renewed tension. She had escaped Colette's recognition, only to find Garrick's net tightening.

A few minutes later, Colette made her own graceful departure. As she passed Seraphina, their paths crossing for a fleeting moment, a subtle shift occurred. Colette paused, her head tilting almost imperceptibly. A faint, almost lost expression crossed her face, as if the ghost of a memory had brushed against her. The gaze of her eyes drifted away from Seraphina's face and instead settled upon the appealing fragrance that emanated from the perfume Seraphina had applied.

It's the perfume, Seraphina realised with a sudden, chilling insight. A rare, unique blend that Colette herself had once favoured, a signature scent that Seraphina had deliberately chosen to mimic in her Mrs Vance persona, as a subtle nod to her past, a personal defiance.

Colette didn't recognise Seraphina, but the familiar fragrance, a phantom whisper from their shared past, stirred a vague, unsettling echo. The moment passed, Colette's face hardened into its usual impassivity, and she left, a lingering question in her gaze.

As the drawing-room slowly emptied; the last of the guests finally departing; Lady Montrose's maid approached her mistress, her face a mask of distress. "My Lady," she whispered, her voice barely audible above the rustle of silks, "the small ivory casket from your dressing room… the one with your grandmother's emerald earrings and the amethyst pendant… it's gone."

Lady Montrose gasped, a sharp, choked sound, her hand flying to her mouth, her face paling dramatically. Across the room, oblivious to the new consternation rippling through the hostess and her staff, Seraphina allowed herself a tiny, almost imperceptible smirk. It was a fleeting shadow of satisfaction that played on her lips, gone as quickly as it appeared. She knew Colette, her nimble-fingered associate, hadn't left empty-handed. The game was truly on now, a perilous dance between three cunning players in the heart of Regency London, with stakes far higher than mere jewels…

Garrick's Visit and Eliza's Unveiling

The day after Lady Montrose's tea party, Thomas Garrick was scheduled to visit, and Seraphina's sophisticated home was filled with a symphony of restrained apprehension. Although Seraphina maintained a calm demeanour, Eliza couldn't help but feel a nervous flutter in her stomach. She had taken great care in preparing the drawing-room, guaranteeing that each cushion was fully plumped, every book neatly arranged, and every flower vase filled with freshly picked flowers. She observed Seraphina's subtle preparations – the selection of a demure yet impeccable gown, the careful arrangement of her hair, the almost imperceptible tightening of her resolve.

At precisely ten o'clock, the familiar rap sounded on the door. Aron, who had arrived earlier, met Garrick in the hall, his presence a quiet, formidable barrier. "Mr Garrick," Aron greeted smoothly, " My wife is expecting you. If you would follow me."

Seraphina rose gracefully as Garrick entered the drawing-room, her smile warm and welcoming. "Mr Garrick, how delightful to see you again. Do excuse me for not having the time to speak with you at Lady Montrose'; it was rather crowded, was it not?" Her voice was light, a subtle mockery of his earlier, terse departure.

Garrick, though he appreciated the subtle jab, remained outwardly unruffled. "Mrs Vance," he replied, his gaze sweeping the room, lingering for a fraction on Eliza, who sat quietly by the window, feigning absorption in a book. "And Mr Vance. My apologies for the imposition, but a matter of some importance requires my attention."

He settled into the armchair Seraphina offered, his posture relaxed, yet his eyes missed nothing. "I am, as you know, investigating a series of perplexing thefts that have plagued London's elite gatherings. Your name, or rather, your previous association with the 'Cavendish Collection' exhibition, has naturally arisen in my inquiries."

Seraphina maintained her composure perfectly. "Indeed? How fascinating. As you recall, Inspector, we merely facilitated the exhibition on behalf of Mr Alistair Cavendish, a most eccentric, if brilliant, collector. A truly unique legacy, now scattered amongst discerning hands."

Garrick nodded. "Remarkable. And your sudden emergence as philanthropists, Mrs Vance, coinciding with this newfound inheritance... it is quite the tale. You must forgive a Bow Street Runner's curiosity, but such shifts in fortune are rare, and often... attract attention." He began to ask seemingly innocuous questions: details about their "family" in Bristol, the precise nature of the late cousin's business, the exact date of their arrival in London as Mr and Mrs Vance. Seraphina wove her well-rehearsed narrative flawlessly, answers polished and consistent, never faltering, never betraying the elaborate fiction. Aron chimed in occasionally, lending his quiet, authoritative support.

Garrick's gaze sharpened as the conversation shifted. He inclined his head, and with a measured calm, pressed further. "And what of the recent thefts—necklaces gone missing, and rumours that a string of incidents followed your arrival in town? Surely a coincidence too convenient to ignore." Seraphina met his stare with unflinching poise, guiding the tale with practiced ease, each detail deliberate; each aside carefully calibrated to deflect scrutiny without lying outright.

Meanwhile, Eliza, listening from her vantage point, felt a nascent discomfort. She had heard these stories before, of course, from Seraphina herself, presented as gentle confidences about her past. But now, under Garrick's polite yet probing questions, Eliza's sharp, newly honed observational skills picked at the edges of Seraphina's perfect narrative.

Bristol? Seraphina had sometimes let slip anecdotes about her youth in a charming country village, never specifically Bristol. 'A reclusive tea merchant's cousin? Seraphina's knowledge of the intricate world of London's art market and high society was far too vast, too intimate, for someone who had just emerged from a provincial obscurity. And her hands, Eliza noticed, though perfectly manicured, bore faint, almost imperceptible calluses that spoke not of a life of leisure, but of meticulous, repetitive work. Eliza thought of the "dexterity exercises" Seraphina had taught her, the subtle manipulation of coins and brooches.

Then, Seraphina made a casual reference to a particular obscure Parisian antique dealer, citing him as a source for one of the Cavendish pieces. Eliza remembered Seraphina mentioning this very dealer days ago, but attributing the knowledge to a passage in a dusty art history book. The discrepancy was tiny, fleeting, but Eliza's mind, now trained to spot such details, registered it.

As Garrick continued his polite interrogation, his voice a steady drone, Eliza found herself seeing Seraphina not just as her benevolent patroness, but as a meticulously constructed performance. The grace, the charm, the seemingly effortless perfection – it was all too precise.

A chill settled over Eliza. She noticed the subtle, almost invisible stitches in Seraphina's flawless tapestry, hints of the elaborate deception that lay beneath the velvet surface. The thought was terrifying, exhilarating, and utterly bewildering. She was no longer just an observer; she was, in fact, a participant in 'Seraphina's Elaborate World of *Deception*.'

Eliza's Perilous Secret

The visit from Garrick had been a chilling revelation for Eliza Beaumont. The polite questions, Seraphina's unwavering composure, and the almost imperceptible inconsistencies; Eliza's newly sharpened senses now detected – it all coalesced into a terrifying understanding. Seraphina was not merely a generous patroness; she was a master of elaborate deceptions, a weaver of intricate lies. Eliza knew with dreadful certainty that if Garrick, with his quiet intensity, ever uncovered that truth, her fate would be irrevocably linked to Seraphina's. The gallows, a chilling prospect for any London criminal, loomed large in her terrified imagination.

The gratitude Eliza had once felt for Seraphina curdled into a potent fear. Her comfortable room, the soft gowns, the nourishing food – they no longer felt like a blessing but a gilded cage. She was an unwitting accomplice, a polished tool in Seraphina's hands, and the thought clawed at her waking hours and haunted her dreams. She had to escape.

Over the next few months, Eliza embarked on a meticulous secret mission. Every shilling of her generous allowance, every small coin Seraphina gave her for errands, was squirrelled away. She bartered skilfully with tradesmen for small commissions, offering to mend fine lace or transcribe elegant invitations for a pittance, then hoarding the proceeds. She became a phantom of thriftiness, her polite refusal of new ribbons or trivial treats baffling the household staff. Her aim was clear: enough money to secure lodgings in a respectable, distant town, enough to live modestly, but freely, away from the glittering, dangerous web she found herself entangled in.

She planned her escape with the same methodical precision Seraphina had instilled in her for observing society's subtle currents. She pored over dusty, leather-bound timetables for the various coaching inns – the *'Swan with Two Necks,'* the *'Belle Sauvage,'* the *'Saracen's Head.'* Her fingers traced routes to Bath and Brighton, memorising departure times, the changing of horses, and the likely duration of each arduous journey. She imagined the biting wind of the open road, the jostle of the carriage, each jolt a severance from her past.

In the quiet solitude of her room, she thought of new identities, not with silks and threads, but with fragments of forgotten names and imagined histories. A distant cousin, come to visit ailing relatives in a quiet market town. A widow seeking solace in a seaside villa. New beginnings, fresh and unburdened, took shape in her mind. Hope, cold and practical, devoid of romantic whimsy, ready to replace the suffocating grip she felt. It was not a soaring, joyous hope, but a steady flicker, fuelled by the prospect of distance and anonymity.

But while Eliza plotted her liberation, a shadow from her past was drawing closer. Her uncle, a man whose rapacious gambling debts had driven her from the countryside, had not forgotten her. He had quietly, relentlessly, pursued whispers of her whereabouts through his own unsavoury contacts, piecing together fragments of information until he discovered his niece, the girl he'd intended to marry off for profit, was living in luxury under the protection of the burgeoning philanthropist, 'Mrs Vance.' A new, far more lucrative scheme fermented in his avaricious mind.

One blustery October afternoon, Eliza ventured out alone. Seraphina was attending a private viewing at a gallery, and Aron was on one of his inscrutable 'business' trips. Eliza had seized the opportunity, ostensibly to visit a small haberdashery, but truly to finalise arrangements for her imminent departure. She clutched the small, heavy coin purse hidden beneath her cloak, the weight of her freedom almost palpable.

As she turned down a narrow, relatively deserted alleyway, a shadow detached itself from the grimy brickwork. Before Eliza could utter a cry, a rough hand clamped over her mouth, another seizing her arm. A wave of sickening recognition washed over her as she stared into the rheumy, triumph-filled eyes of her uncle. He reeked of cheap gin and desperation.

"Well, well, my little songbird," he rasped, his voice a gravelly whisper that sent a shiver of ice down Eliza's spine. His grip, when it closed around her arm, was like iron, bruising and inescapable. "Found yourself a fine new nest, haven't we? Don't worry, your dear patroness will ensure you're returned... for a price."

Eliza struggled, her heart hammering against her ribs like a trapped bird, but his brutish strength was overwhelming. He pulled her unceremoniously into a waiting, unkempt hackney coach, its interior reeking of stale straw, damp wool, and something vaguely metallic. The door slammed shut with a sickening thud, plunging her into an abrupt, suffocating darkness. As she peered through the grimy and smeared window, her last glimpse was of the familiar, elegant street, where Seraphina's imposing townhouse was now receding into the distance. Her hard-won freedom, so recently tasted, dissolved into the murky London haze, leaving behind only the chilling certainty of impending dread...

Ransome

Back at Seraphina's house, a harsh intrusion marred the pristine oak of the front door: a small, grimy note, impaled with a rusty nail, declaring its presence with an almost brutal finality. Aron, returning later that afternoon, discovered it. His face, usually a study in impassive calm, tightened almost imperceptibly as he read the crudely scrawled, menacing script.

113

"To the esteemed Mrs Vance," it began, the words themselves oozing a malevolent familiarity. "Your little songbird has flown. A most precious pet. If you wish for her safe return, a sum of ten thousand guineas will secure her. Deliver to the old wharf, south dock, at midnight, two nights hence. Come alone. Any intervention, any Bow Street interference, and your bird sings her last tune."

Aron's jaw clenched, a muscle working furiously as he crumpled the note into a tight, unforgiving ball. Eliza, their unwitting pawn in a far grander scheme, was gone. And her desperate, grasping uncle had just thrown a most inconvenient and dangerous wrench into their meticulously orchestrated lives.

An Unholy Alliance

The ransom note lay crumpled on Seraphina's elegant desk, a crude, violent stain on the polished surface of her meticulously crafted life. Eliza. Gone. The single word resonated with a chilling finality. The fear that snaked through Seraphina was not just for the girl herself, though a flicker of genuine concern for the innocent pawn stirred within her, a brief, unwelcome warmth. No, the true terror was the chilling understanding of the threat Eliza now posed. The girl had observed too much, learned too much, even unwittingly. If her desperate uncle extracted information from her, or if she simply broke under the pressure, their entire intricate deception, their very lives, would unravel, leaving them exposed and vulnerable.

"We have no choice, Aron," Seraphina stated, her voice tight, devoid of its usual silken calm, each word a carefully measured weight. "We cannot risk what Eliza knows falling into the wrong hands. And a direct confrontation with a desperate man is messy, unpredictable. It leaves traces." The unspoken consequences hung heavy in the air between them.

Aron, his face grim, nodded slowly, his gaze fixed on the crumpled paper, as if willing it to disappear. He understood the stakes with painful clarity. To go to Garrick, the relentless investigator who suspected them most, was to walk directly into the lion's den, to lay bare a sliver of their vulnerability. But the alternative – a potential breach of their entire operation, the very foundation of their existence – was utterly unacceptable.

"He will demand answers," Aron warned, his voice a low rumble, the words a palpable obstacle.

"And we shall give him answers," Seraphina countered, a dangerous, calculating glint entering her eyes, a predatory spark that promised more than it revealed. "We will give enough to gain his cooperation; not enough to condemn ourselves." The tension in the room coiled taut and electric as two brilliant minds plotted their most audacious gamble yet.

The next morning, under the persistent veil of a fine drizzle, the polished wheels of their private carriage splashed through the grime of Bow Street, drawing to a halt before the unpretentious brick facade of the Runners' office. Seraphina, draped in a travelling cloak of deep forest green that barely concealed the exquisite silk beneath, stepped out, a study in elegant contrast against the grim, bustling thoroughfare. Aron followed, his tall frame adding to their almost theatrical presence.

Inside, the air hung heavy with the scent of damp wool, stale pipe smoke, and the faint, metallic tang of unwashed humanity. Garrick's clerk, a harried man with ink-stained fingers, led them through a narrow passage, past a cacophony of hushed interviews and the scratching of quills, to Garrick's own office. It was a stark, almost monastic chamber: a scarred wooden desk, two straight-backed chairs, and a single, grime-streaked window offering a view of a perpetually grey sky. Garrick himself looked up from a stack of dispatches, his spectacles perched on the end of his nose. His expression, usually so quick to betray amusement or suspicion, remained utterly unreadable. No surprise, no hint of triumph, merely a quiet, assessing gaze that seemed to acknowledge their audacious presence without fanfare.

"Mrs Vance," Garrick greeted, his gaze flicking to Aron. "And Mr Vance. To what do I owe this... unexpected visit?"

Seraphina's poise was steady, though a hint of genuine distress coloured her voice. "Sir, we find ourselves in a most regrettable predicament.

Our companion, Miss Eliza Beaumont, a young woman under our protection, has been… abducted."

Garrick's brows rose. "Indeed? And what leads you to this conclusion?" Aron placed the crude ransom note on Garrick's desk. "This note was left on our door. Her uncle, a desperate man with severe gambling debts, has discovered her whereabouts. He demands ten thousand guineas for her safe return."

Garrick picked up the note, his eyes scanning the rough script, then slowly looked up, his gaze piercing. "Ten thousand guineas, Mr Vance? That is a considerable sum for a 'companion.' And this 'uncle'… what does Miss Beaumont know that makes her worth such a price?"

Seraphina met his gaze directly. "Eliza, Mr Garrick, comes from a family with… delicate connections. Her knowledge of certain family affairs, which we now oversee because of a sudden inheritance, could be highly detrimental if it fell into unscrupulous hands. Her uncle, we suspect, believes this information holds far greater value than it truly does, yet the threat remains. We fear for her safety, and for the unfortunate scandal such a revelation could cause amongst our, and by extension, the Duchess's, associates."

It was a brilliant lie, interwoven with just enough truth – the "sudden inheritance," the "delicate connections" to high society – to be plausible. It implied a vulnerability, a legitimate reason for a ransom, without hinting at their true, illicit activities.

Garrick leant back in his chair, a slow, calculating look spreading across his face. "So, you wish for the Bow Street Runners to intervene, to risk an armed confrontation for a private family matter?" He was testing them, assessing their desperation.

"We wish for the innocent girl's safe return," Seraphina stated, her voice imbued with a quiet, yet firm, conviction. "And for this man to be apprehended before he causes further mischief. We believe that a combined effort would be most efficient." The implication hung in the air: 'You need an arrest, Inspector, and we need this problem solved discreetly.'

A tense silence filled the room. Garrick finally nodded, a flicker of grudging respect in his eyes. This was a direct line into the very heart of the 'Vance's" operation, even if they were only offering a carefully curated glimpse. He might not get the full truth, but he would get Eliza, and potentially, a leverage point. "Very well," he said, his voice decisive. "Midnight, south dock. My men will be there. Discreetly, of course."...

The old wharf at the south dock was a desolate, forgotten place under the oppressive shroud of midnight, a sinister expanse where shadows clung to every rotting timber and the air hung heavy with the cloying stench of low tide, stale fish, and desperate hope. Garrick's men, seasoned and silent, positioned themselves with surgical precision; they were dark, predatory shadows among the skeletal remains of old rigging, the looming hulks of decaying ships, and the haphazard stacks of abandoned, brine-soaked crates.

Seraphina and Aron stood in the agreed-upon, desolate spot, their figures stark and vulnerable against the flickering, melancholic light of a distant gas lamp that seemed only to deepen the surrounding gloom. Seraphina held a heavy satchel, its weight a cruel deception – filled not with the full, exorbitant ransom, but with strategically placed weights beneath a thin, mocking layer of genuine banknotes.

At the stroke of midnight, a deeper shadow detached itself from the inky blackness. The uncle emerged from the gloom, a grotesque silhouette, dragging a struggling, terrified Eliza behind him. Her slight form was a pathetic counterpoint to his hulking frame, her eyes, wide with a terror that transcended mere fear, locked onto Seraphina. "The money!" the uncle rasped, his voice slurred with drink and a desperation that bordered on madness. "Hand it over, or the girl takes a swim!" He punctuated his threat with a jarring tug on Eliza's arm, eliciting a small, choked whimper.

Seraphina moved forward, her composure a shield against the rising tide of fear. She slid the heavy satchel across the grimy planks, the faint rasping sound unnaturally loud in the oppressive silence. "The girl first," she commanded, her voice cutting through the tension with an icy authority, brooking no argument.

As the uncle, his eyes gleaming with avarice, lunged greedily for the bag, a whistle, sharp and piercing, tore through the suffocating silence of the night. Suddenly, as if conjured from the very shadows, figures materialised – Garrick's runners, a disciplined force of retribution. The uncle, momentarily stunned, his focus fractured, loosened his grip on Eliza. In that fleeting instant, Eliza stumbled free, a fragile, desperate bird taking flight, and ran directly into Aron's waiting, protective arms.

"Bow Street Runners! Get him!" Garrick's voice, booming and authoritative, shattered the stillness, echoing across the silent docks as his men surged forward. They moved with swift efficiency, apprehending the wildly cursing uncle, who snarled and spat, a trapped animal caught in a snare, his desperate gamble finally, irrevocably, lost.

In the ensuing chaos, amidst the shouts of the runners and the uncle's guttural curses, Seraphina's eyes met Garrick's across the grimy expanse of the dock. It was a silent acknowledgement, a fleeting, almost imperceptible exchange that transcended the cacophony. Eliza was safe, tucked away, trembling but unharmed, in Aron's arms. They apprehended the uncle, a snarling, pathetic figure. But in that brief, intense gaze, a profound, uneasy understanding passed between Garrick and Seraphina. The alliance, born of desperate necessity, had been forged, and in its fiery crucible, the once-clear lines between hunter and hunted had blurred irrevocably.

As Garrick, his gaze lingering on Seraphina for a fraction too long, led away the struggling, spitting uncle, Seraphina knew with chilling certainty that their meticulously guarded secret had gained a powerful, dangerous new layer. Their velvet deception, woven with such exquisite care, was now known to the very man sworn to expose them. And in that shared knowledge, that unspoken complicity, lay the tantalising promise of a game far more intricate, and infinitely more perilous, than any they had played before. The hunt, it seemed, had only just begun.

Chapter 7

The Chessboard Shifts

The private viewing room of Lord Harrington's London residence was thick with the scent of aged mahogany and unctuous flattery. 'Seraphina Vance', radiant in a gown of midnight blue, was in the midst of orchestrating a delicate deception. Their target: Sir Byron Finch *(no relation to their solicitor),* a man whose immense wealth was matched only by his even more immense vanity and his fervent, yet utterly uneducated, belief in his own connoisseurship. The current play presented a seemingly authentic but subtly flawed snuffbox, and Finch believed it to be a lost masterpiece. Seraphina's role was to confirm his "discovery," subtly elevate its perceived value, and then, through a series of carefully managed 'expert' opinions, arrange its sale at an inflated price, allowing them to pocket a tidy commission on a highly profitable, if entirely fabricated, transaction.

Eliza, now pale and quiet after her ordeal, watched from a discreet distance, nominally serving tea, but her eyes darting nervously. Her mind was a whirlwind of fear and dawning comprehension. The terrifying rescue had shattered the illusion of Seraphina's benevolent perfection, exposing the dangerous currents beneath. She was still under Seraphina's roof, and the recent events with Garrick meant she was more entangled than ever.

Seraphina, however, was in her element. She held the snuffbox with reverence, turning it slowly in her gloved hands. "Sir Byron," she purred, her voice a low, appreciative murmur, "the craftsmanship is simply sublime. The way the light catches the enamel… a true testament to the Georgian era. One could almost believe it was from the very workshop of Faberge himself, were it not for its subtle... 'provincial charm'."

Finch, preening, puffed out his chest. "Ah yes, Mrs Vance! My own discerning eye, you see! I discovered it at a most unexpected curiosity shop!"

Just as Seraphina was about to launch into the delicate phase of suggesting a 'reputable' expert who would 'confirm' Finch's genius (and her inflated valuation), an unfamiliar figure entered the viewing room. Madame Colette Delacroix. She moved with almost predatory grace, her eyes sharp and calculating, sweeping the room before settling, with chilling precision, on the snuffbox in Seraphina's hands. Colette's impeccably dressed figure, in a simple yet exquisitely tailored black gown, starkly contrasted with the room's opulence, giving her an air of formidable authority.

"Ah, Madame Delacroix!" Lord Harrington, the host, boomed, his voice a jovial thunderclap that seemed utterly oblivious to the subtle, almost imperceptible shift in the room's carefully constructed atmosphere. "A delight to see you once again, my dear lady, so glad you accepted my invitation. I am told you possess a supreme eye for true artistry, a connoisseur without equal!"

Colette offered a curt, almost dismissive nod to Harrington, her lips barely curving into what might pass for a smile. Her gaze, sharp and unblinking, remained fixed, not on the effusive host, but on the delicate snuffbox cradled in Seraphina's hand. Then, with a chilling deliberation that seemed to draw all the air from the room, she glided towards Seraphina. Her movements were slow, fluid, unnervingly precise, like a viper approaching its prey, every coil of its body imbued with lethal intent. Seraphina's blood ran cold, a prickling sensation that started at her nape and spread rapidly, an icy premonition of danger.

"An interesting piece," Colette stated, her voice cool, melodic, devoid of any warmth. Her eyes, those same piercing eyes that had once scrutinised Seraphina's every move in her employ, now held a chillingly familiar glint. "Though," she continued, picking up the snuffbox from Seraphina's startled hand, her fingers brushing Seraphina's in a fleeting, unnerving contact, "the enamel work, while commendable, reveals a rather telltale 'micro-fissure' near the base of the lid. A common fault in provincial reproductions of the period. And the hallmark... a clever forgery, but not quite perfect under a certain light."

The words hung in the air like poison. Finch's face, minutes ago beaming with self-importance, crumpled into a mask of confusion and dawning humiliation. He snatched the snuffbox from Colette's hand, peering at it, then at Seraphina, a nascent suspicion in his gaze. Colette's interference was direct, devastating, designed to utterly unravel Seraphina's credit, to expose her as a purveyor of fakes. The operation was seconds from collapsing, taking Seraphina's meticulously built reputation with it.

A cold, visceral fear pierced through Seraphina, but a surge of pure, unadulterated defiance quickly eclipsed it. Had Collette recognised Seraphina? If so, was this Colette's cruel game, a public humiliation disguised as an astute observation.

Seraphina's mind raced, recalling Colette's own teachings: *When cornered, embrace the truth, but twist its meaning."*

"Ah, Madame Delacroix," Seraphina said, her voice betraying not a hint of panic, but a profound, almost sorrowful, understanding. She reached out, retrieving the snuffbox, turning it to catch the light. "Your eyes, I must say, are unparalleled. You have indeed spotted the micro-fissure." She paused, letting Finch's growing horror settle.

"But that, Sir Byron," Seraphina continued, her voice dropping to a conspiratorial whisper, drawing Finch in, "is precisely the 'genius of this piece! It is not, as Madame Delacroix correctly observes, a flawless masterwork. It is, in fact, a remarkably astute, and extremely rare, *'contemporary forgery'* from the period, created by an artisan so skilled they mimicked not just the style, but also the 'common flaws' of the true master, to fool lesser collectors!"

She spun the tale with breathtaking speed, improvising on the spot. "The brilliance lies in its very imperfection, its meta-deception! This makes it even rarer than the original. Think of it, a master forger so audacious, he copied the very errors! It is a collector's ultimate secret, a piece that only truly discerning eyes, like your own, Sir Byron, and perhaps Madame Delacroix's, would appreciate for its unique historical significance as a 'study' in Georgian fraud!"

Finch, his vanity bruised but now intrigued by this new, even more 'clever' interpretation, wavered. Colette, watching from a short distance, a faint, almost imperceptible smirk playing on her lips, saw Seraphina's desperate improvisation. Her eyes, meeting Seraphina's for a fleeting second, held a chilling blend of grudging respect and simmering vengeance. There was no recognition of the girl she knew, but a silent declaration of war between two formidable adversaries.

"Remarkable," Colette purred, her eyes still fixed on Seraphina, the "familiar perfume" from the tea party now an almost tangible scent of past betrayal in the room. Her words were for Finch, but her gaze was a challenge to Seraphina. "A most… 'unconventional' interpretation. One that requires a truly daring intellect to conceive." The double meaning was clear.

Sir Byron, convinced anew by Seraphina's dazzling improvisation and his own inflated ego, now saw the snuffbox not as a damaged piece, but as a unique anomaly of historical deception. The ploy was saved, but at a cost. Seraphina had revealed an additional layer of her cunning to Colette, a desperate improvisation born of necessity. The chessboard had indeed shifted, and Seraphina knew, with a cold certainty, that Colette's appearance was no accident. The mentor had thrown down the gauntlet, and the game had turned from mere profit to a perilous, silent war of wits, fuelled by an old, bitter score. -

Apex of Audacity

As Seraphina paced her study, Colette Delacroix's brazen interference at Lord Harrington's still infuriated her. The calculated contempt in Colette's eyes, a chilling echo of their shared past, confirmed Seraphina's fears—this wasn't just a reappearance; it was a declaration of war. Colette sought to dismantle Seraphina's life piece by piece, a threat that demanded an equally audacious response.

Seraphina's plan was simple: she needed a swindle so grand it would not only replenish her resources and bolster her burgeoning reputation but also serve as an irresistible snare for Colette. Her target was the Duke of Rutland, a man whose greed was as legendary as his corruption.

"The Duke of Rutland is a viper," Seraphina informed Aron, her voice devoid of emotion as she paced her study. "He has amassed a fortune through bribery, smuggling, and exploiting the poor. And he has a particular weakness: a desire for an unblemished reputation, especially regarding his 'charitable' endeavours, to ease his entry into the Queen's privy council."

Seraphina and Aron concocted a masterpiece of misdirection, a scheme as brilliant as the illusions they sold. Their target was the Duke of Rutland, a man whose immense wealth was matched only by his desperate hunger for cultural prestige.

They would offer him a "lost" Elizabethan masterpiece—a painting whose scandalous royal associations had kept it hidden for centuries. The painting itself was a breathtaking forgery, crafted with painstaking detail by an ailing, reclusive artist Seraphina had been patronising for months. Its true value wasn't in its authenticity, but in the duke's insatiable desire for history and prestige. He would willingly pay a fortune for the piece, blissfully unaware of his role in their grand deception.

The audacious part, however, the truly venomous twist in their intricate plot, was the method of delivery – a meticulously crafted false trail designed to implicate Colette. Seraphina wanted her old association with Madame Colette, a ghost from a past she desperately wished to bury, out of her life permanently. This wasn't merely about profit; it was about severance, about finally cutting the last, lingering thread that bound her to a world she had so painstakingly escaped.

The forged painting's provenance would be subtly yet undeniably linked to known 'discreet' contacts Colette notoriously used for her own illicit art dealings. Every fabricated document, every whispered rumour, every carefully placed clue would ensure the scent of the swindle, the stink of the deception, led directly and unequivocally to Colette, leaving Seraphina and Aron untouched, their hands clean, their reputations pristine, and their past finally, irrevocably, severed…

Eliza, meanwhile, was being drawn deeper, irreversibly deeper, into the glittering, treacherous vortex of Seraphina's world. Her unease was a palpable thing, a constant, low thrum beneath her carefully polished manner, a tremor that threatened to shatter her composure with every passing day. She was no longer just an observer, a quiet presence in the opulent rooms; she had become an unwitting 'courier and decoy', a pawn in a game whose rules she barely understood but whose stakes she instinctively felt were terrifyingly high.

Despite her gratitude to Seraphina for rescuing her, Eliza was terrified. Each innocent errand—delivering silk-wrapped packages of forged documents—deepened her fear of being caught. The coded instructions and clandestine routes made it clear she was an accomplice in a dangerous charade, and the thought of being unmasked and hanged for her part in the deception became a constant, gnawing dread.

She hated the life she had become involved with, hated the constant tension, the lies, the fear of every shadow. She felt trapped, a gilded bird in a cage of Seraphina's making, desperate to escape but with no idea how to find the key. The gratitude warred with a simmering loathing, a toxic brew that left her teetering on the precipice of despair.

While Seraphina set her grand trap, Thomas Garrick felt an almost visceral connection to his quarry. The 'Vance's' were proving more elusive than any criminal he'd ever pursued. The Eliza Beaumont incident, however, had given him invaluable insight. He now knew they had vulnerabilities, and that Seraphina, despite her iron composure, possessed a human element he could exploit. The ransom payment, even if a fraction of the demand, spoke volumes.

His investigation had intensified, shifting from a quiet hum of suspicion to a relentless, all-consuming drive. He had discreetly shadowed Eliza since her return, a shadow among shadows, noting every anxious glance, every subtle, telling change in her routine. Her very discomfort was a beacon, guiding him closer to the truth. Beyond Eliza, his network of informants had confirmed his growing unease. He had assigned men, his most trusted and unobtrusive, to keep a low profile around the Duke of Rutland's estate, a sprawling nexus of old money and new ambition. The duke's sudden, uncharacteristic, almost feverish interest in "historical pieces" had not just piqued Garrick's suspicion; it had screamed an alarm.

As whispers of a "lost Elizabethan masterpiece" reached Garrick's ears, an icy dread settled in his gut. The rumours sounded exactly like the kind of scheme Seraphina would orchestrate. What was more, this

131

"Madame Colette Delacroix" he had just met—what was her connection to all this?

"Miller," Garrick commanded, his voice a low rumble. He traced a web of shadowed alleys while hunched over a map. "Investigate every known associate of Madame Colette Delacroix. I want to know about any recent, unusual items arriving from Paris, especially anything related to illicit art sales. And watch the Duke of Rutland's acquisitions with the utmost scrutiny. These two narratives," he said, his gaze hardening, "are far too intertwined for coincidence. I have a very bad gut feeling."

The following day, a sense of urgency prickled at Garrick. He needed to understand the intricate machinery of Seraphina Vance's operations, the true nature of her "business," and the extent of Eliza Beaumont's involvement. He had observed a subtle yet profound shift in Eliza – a new skittishness, a haunted look in her eyes that spoke volumes. Garrick, a keen observer of human nature, a man who could read the unwritten anxieties on a person's face, suspected Eliza was no longer the innocent victim she first appeared. Her terror was genuine, but it was now laced with complicity.

He sent one of his most trusted female operatives, a woman named Tilly Proctor, as adept at extracting secrets as she was at blending into the shadows. Tilly, disguised as a distant, impoverished relative seeking charity, was dispatched to gain Eliza's confidence. Garrick gambled that Eliza's palpable fear, her growing desperation, would be the crack in

Seraphina's formidable defences, the weak point through which he could finally expose the truth. He wanted to know how deep the rabbit hole went, and Eliza, he was certain, held the key.

Meanwhile, Seraphina, a predator in her prime, poised to execute her most audacious swindle yet, meticulously laid a trap for her former mentor, Colette. Every detail was a poisoned barb, every calculated step designed to ensnare. And Eliza, a fragile, unwitting decoy, moved pieces across a chessboard she barely comprehended, her every innocent action unknowingly tightening the noose around Seraphina's intended victim. And Garrick, driven by an unyielding sense of justice, a burning conviction that transcended mere duty, and a deep-seated suspicion that prickled at the back of his neck like a storm approaching, edged ever closer.

With chilling clarity, he was certain that the Duke of Rutland's latest, much-vaunted acquisition would be the key, the final, undeniable proof needed to finally expose Seraphina Vance and dismantle her glittering empire of deceit...

The Bait and The Whisper

The air in the Duke of Rutland's private study was thick with the scent of old money and avarice. The duke, a man of immense girth and even greater greed, stood before a draped easel, his eyes gleaming with barely contained excitement. Beside him, Seraphina projected an aura of confident mastery, her expression a careful blend of deference and subtle power. For Eliza, positioned near the fireplace with a teacup rattling in her trembling hand, the moment was a delicate dance on a razor's edge. One wrong move, and Seraphina's masterful deception—a con built on stolen secrets—would crumble.

"The history of this piece, Your Grace," Seraphina began, her voice a low, melodic hum, "is as rich as its hues. Hidden for centuries, its rediscovery through the most unconventional channels is nothing short of miraculous." With a dramatic flourish, Aron, her silent accomplice, unveiled the painting. The "masterpiece" was indeed breathtaking: a vibrant portrait of a Tudor lady, rendered with a patina of age that spoke of centuries in a forgotten vault. The duke gasped, his jowls quivering with delight. The promise of not just wealth, but true cultural prestige entranced him.

Meanwhile, while Seraphina was entertaining the duke - a discrete figure moved silently through the outer receiving rooms. This was 'Madame Colette Delacroix', a legendary architect of deception herself. Seraphina had painstakingly planted subtle, untraceable clues—veiled references to old Parisian contacts, breadcrumbs she knew would lead her discerning rival straight to the promised score. Colette, following the scent of the swindle, curiosity battling with a cold fury, slipped into a hidden alcove she knew well from past dealings in this very house. From her perch, she watched the unfolding drama.

As the Duke admired his new acquisition, Seraphina launched into the painting's fabricated provenance, a silky narrative of reclusive collectors, daring escapes during the French Revolution, and clandestine art recovery agents. Each detail was a subtle, calculated echo of Colette's own signature methods and associates—her very fingerprint on the illicit art world. This wasn't just a story; it was a deliberate and unmistakable imitation of the techniques Colette had once taught her.

A polished silver box slipped from Aron's hand, clattering loudly on the floor—a pre-arranged diversion. In the split second of distraction, Eliza moved with feigned alarm to retrieve it. As she bent, she deftly let a small, intricately carved jade ring—one Colette had gifted to Seraphina years ago—fall from her sleeve. It was a subtle, almost imperceptible clue, a signature of the past.

Colette, hidden in an alcove, saw the familiar ring and her eyes narrowed. This wasn't just a swindle; it was a taunt. Seraphina was using the very methods Colette herself had taught her, and now she was leaving behind a calling card. Her sardonic smile vanished, replaced by a chilling, absolute clarity. This was a trap, a challenge thrown down with exquisite precision, designed to entangle her in Seraphina's grand deception.

A flicker of cold amusement, quick as a viper's strike, crossed Colette's features, swiftly followed by an incandescent rage. Her old apprentice, the timid girl she had sculpted from raw ambition, had blossomed into her most dangerous rival. Every lesson, every nuance of the con, was now a weapon aimed squarely at her. This was not a disagreement; this was war. Colette did not intervene. She remained a silent, unmoving sentinel, her eyes like polished obsidian, fixed on the unfolding scene, already calculating her inevitable counter-move. The duke, meanwhile, scrawled his signature with a flourish, utterly unaware that the intricate, deadly deception tightening its coils around him was only the beginning...

Garrick's Persistent Shadow

Previously, Garrick's meticulously placed operative, Tilly Proctor, was making headway with Eliza Beaumont. Disguised as 'Miss Davies,' a distant cousin seeking advice on charitable ventures, Tilly had cultivated a polite acquaintance with Eliza over several weeks, bumping into her on carefully orchestrated 'chance' encounters.

One blustery afternoon, Tilly found Eliza sitting alone in a quiet corner of Hyde Park, sketching a telltale melancholic air about her. The rescue from her uncle had left Eliza shaken, and the constant, subtle deceptions she was now privy to chipped away at her fragile sense of security.

"Miss Beaumont," Tilly began, her voice warm and solicitous, "a pleasure to encounter you again. You seem... thoughtful today."

Eliza sighed, a quiet, almost imperceptible sound. "Indeed, Miss Davies. London can be a bewildering place, can it not? So many faces, so many... layers."

Tilly leaned closer, her voice dropping to a conspiratorial whisper. "It can indeed. Especially when one finds oneself in new circumstances, surrounded by grand expectations. My dear cousin, while a kind soul, has rather eccentric habits, and I often feel adrift. One longs for a guiding hand, but sometimes, I wonder who truly holds the rudder." She watched Eliza closely; a subtle seed of doubt planted in her words.

Eliza's eyes, wide and troubled, met Tilly's. "You speak of layers," she murmured, her voice barely audible. "Sometimes, Miss Davies, I fear the layers are so deep one can no longer discern what lies beneath." Seeking a connection, a way to share her silent terror, she hesitated before adding, "My own situation has become rather more complicated than I ever expected."

Tilly's heart quickened. This was it. The crack. "Complicated, my dear? How so? Perhaps a sympathetic ear could ease your burden. My experience with certain *unconventional* family situations has taught me that often, a quiet word to the right person can avert great sorrow." She carefully avoided direct questions, allowing Eliza to volunteer the information, building trust with empathy.

137

Eliza looked around, as if fearing eavesdroppers, though the park was relatively empty. "It is not merely family, Miss Davies," she whispered, her gaze distant, fixed on the bare branches overhead. "It is the very ground I walk on. I fear... I fear I am treading on thin ice, and that the thaw may be imminent."

Later that evening, as gaslights flickered across London, Garrick received Tilly's discreet report. Her words, delivered with quiet precision, confirmed his suspicions and sparked a grim satisfaction within him. He wasn't just getting fragments of information; he was gaining access to the very heart of Seraphina's meticulously constructed world. The impenetrable walls around her were beginning to show hairline cracks, fissures that promised to widen under the right pressure.

Eliza Beaumont, the unwitting pawn in Seraphina's grand game, was on the verge of singing like a bird. Tilly's careful cultivation of Eliza's trust, her patient understanding of the young woman's terror and desperation, was bearing fruit. Eliza's fragile composure was crumbling, and soon, Garrick knew, she would become a vital witness, a conduit to the truth that Seraphina so desperately sought to bury.

The game, once confined to Seraphina's machinations, had escalated, involving not two, but three master players: Seraphina, the audacious puppeteer; Colette, the cunning, wounded mentor; and himself, Garrick, the relentless pursuer of justice. And now, a fourth unwitting participant: Eliza, caught in the perilous crossfire. The stakes were higher; the tension unbearable. The climax, dangerous and inevitable, was rapidly approaching.

Eliza's Confession: A Whisper in the Park

The afternoon sun filtered through the leaves in Hyde Park, but for Eliza, it cast a long, cold shadow. The fear that had been her constant companion was finally beginning to crumble her carefully built defences. Across from her, Tilly, posing as the kind and empathetic 'Miss Davies,' offered a sympathetic ear that was all Eliza had desperately craved. The relentless pressure of Seraphina's deceptive world, the terror of her uncle's brutal interrogation, had pushed Eliza to her breaking point. Tilly's calm presence was the release she sought, the one person she felt she could trust with her shattering truth.

"It's not just the layers of deception," Eliza confessed, her voice a fragile whisper, her eyes darting nervously as if the very trees could betray her. "It's the foundation of everything. Nothing is real. Mrs Vance... Seraphina... she is not who she appears to be. Her fortune, her connections, even her name. It's all... a performance."

Tilly remained outwardly calm, her senses on high alert. This information was exactly what Garrick needed. "A performance?" Tilly asked gently, inviting more. "My dear, what could you possibly mean?"

Eliza's secrets finally spilled out in a frantic rush. "The inheritance, the lost cousin in Bristol... it's all fake. I heard her and Mr Aron plan every detail. And the paintings… the 'Cavendish Collection'… I suspect many of them are forgeries. I've seen her examine them with a magnifying glass, pointing out subtle differences in brushwork that she later 'explained' to buyers."

She shuddered, a fresh wave of horror hitting her as she recalled her uncle. "He believed I knew specific details about her wealth, her 'sources.' When he took me, he called her a 'queen of shadows,' a 'mistress of deceit.' I was terrified he would force me to reveal what little I knew. The Bow Street Runners would also implicate me if they uncovered her true dealings. I would be ruined. Or worse." The unspoken word '*hanged*' hung in the air between them, a chilling testament to her fear.

As Eliza's terror-fuelled confession poured forth, Tilly's heart sang. The girl's desperate need for a confidante was providing the very details Garrick needed for a conviction. Every detail Eliza revealed was another thread in the web Seraphina had spun, a web that was now, thanks to Eliza's terrified honesty, beginning to unravel.

Tilly reached out, gently patting Eliza's trembling hand. "My dear, you are an innocent caught in a terrible tangle. You must understand that if what you say is true, you are a victim, not an accomplice. Although the law's reach is extensive, it can differentiate between those who deceive and those who are innocently ensnared." She offered a glimmer of hope, a potential path to safety, if Eliza continued to cooperate.

Later that evening, Thomas Garrick listened to Tilly's detailed report. The raw desperation in Eliza Beaumont's voice, meticulously recounted by his operative, confirmed his deepest suspicions: Seraphina Vance's entire persona was an elaborate lie.

"Eliza confirmed the fabricated inheritance, sir," Tilly stated crisply. "But she offered much more. She spoke of several recent schemes, including a fraudulent charity for war orphans. She also suspects the 'Cavendish' paintings are not genuine, having overheard Seraphina and Aron discussing how they created details and 'authenticated' them for buyers. The girl is terrified of being implicated and fears the gallows. Her fear has made her our most valuable witness."

Garrick, his usual deliberate trudge replaced by a predatory energy, paced his cramped office. A grim satisfaction settled over him as he processed Tilly's report. "Excellent, Tilly," he murmured, "You have done a great job."

He stopped at the grimy window, gazing out at the perpetual drizzle. "Eliza Beaumont is our key. She's seen the cracks, the subtle fissures in Seraphina's foundations. We have enough to bring her in." A flicker of grudging admiration crossed his face. "She's been taught how to look, Tilly, to dissect, to observe, even if she didn't fully comprehend the why."

He understood Eliza's fear; it was a potent, visceral dread that coiled around her. Garrick, who had spent a lifetime observing the darker currents of human nature, knew its power. It was a sharp and uncompromising motivator, and he would use it to pry open the truth and bring about Seraphina's inevitable arrest.

The relationship between Eliza and Tilly now served a critical purpose for Garrick. Tilly was no longer just a sympathetic listener; she was Garrick's direct line into the heart of Seraphina's household. Through Eliza, they could gather details of ongoing operations, anticipate future moves, and, most crucially, find the undeniable evidence needed to make an arrest stick.

However, this new dynamic came with significant consequences for Eliza: she had found a confidante, a fragile hope of escape, but she was now an unwitting informant. Her continued deception, both to Seraphina and now to herself, would be a constant psychological burden. Her life remained steeped in secrecy, with the added pressure of potentially betraying the woman who, despite everything, had saved her from utter destitution.

The threat from her uncle might have passed, but a new, more subtle danger now surrounded her. And for Seraphina: she remained oblivious to Eliza's clandestine meetings with Tilly, trusting in the girl's loyalty and gratitude.

This blind spot was a critical vulnerability Garrick now possessed. Every piece of information Eliza passed to Tilly would be a nail in the coffin of Seraphina's carefully constructed empire. Her greatest strength – her ability to command loyalty and trust – was now also her gravest weakness. For Garrick: He had secured a vital intelligence asset, but it necessitated a delicate touch. He couldn't push Eliza too hard, or she might break, or worse, warn Seraphina. He needed to maintain Tilly's cover and ensure Eliza remained unaware of her true role as an informant. This was a high-stakes gamble, requiring patience and cunning. The game was no longer about tracking individual thefts; it was about an elaborate internal separating.

The confession in the park had shifted the chessboard profoundly. The velvet deception now had a hidden seam, and Garrick held the thread. The question was not if Seraphina's world would unravel, but when, and at what cost to all involved...

A Serpent's Embrace

Seraphina and Aron waited in the Duke of Rutland's private gallery. The "lost Elizabethan masterpiece" hung on the wall, bathed in the soft glow of candlelight. The duke, preening with self-satisfaction, had paid an exorbitant sum for the painting, his vanity blinding him to the deception.

As they sat down to dinner and watched him sign the final transfer papers, a triumphant, almost imperceptible smile played on Seraphina's lips. The audacious swindle was complete. The forged provenance, carefully seeded with subtle references to Colette Delacroix, now pointed an accusatory finger directly at Seraphina's former mentor, leaving Seraphina and Aron completely clean. It was the perfect crime, with the perfect scapegoat.

The duke's butler, his starched collar softening with the late hour, served the final course. Seraphina, needing a moment of air, slipped onto the grand portico. The cool evening breeze was a balm to her heightened senses, and as she gathered her cloak, a deep, resonant satisfaction settled over her. The job was done. With their excuses made, she and Aron left.

The air in the carriage, once thick with the sweet scent of triumph and lavender, turned to ice. Seraphina, her hand still reaching for Aron, froze. The name "Colette" had barely left her lips—a soft, venomous promise—when a voice, sharp and cold as a winter's blade, sliced through the quiet.

"Indeed, Sylvie. And a familiar bag it is."

It wasn't Aron's voice. The soft leather of the carriage seat groaned as Seraphina's head snapped around, her triumphant smile gone, replaced by dawning horror. The carriage door Seraphina had believed sealed and secure was slightly ajar. Standing there, a lone figure silhouetted against the mansion's distant glow, was Colette. The faint light caught her eye, and the familiar lilt of her voice cut through the air, chilling Seraphina to the bone. The situation was not merely a confrontation but something more significant than that.

Both Seraphina and Aron froze, their movements arrested mid-gesture, mid-breath. The air in the carriage, moments before thick with the heady aroma of victory, now crackled with an undeniable, terrifying presence. Seraphina's face, usually a mask of controlled elegance, was now etched with a chilling blend of fury and an unnerving, absolute recognition.

"Go! Drive!" Aron barked, a desperate tremor in his voice as he rapped furiously on the carriage wall. "Drive!" But Colette simply jumped inside, her gaze fixed on Seraphina. Seraphina shoved her, her hands trembling. "Get out! You have no right-"

Colette didn't budge. "But I do," she said, her voice a low, final chord. "You see, you are mine. And I have come for what you stole from me!" Seraphina was furious with an intensity that stripped away years; away the carefully constructed facade, revealing the desperate, ambitious girl who had fled her employ.

"Get out, Colette," Seraphina yelled, her voice remarkably clear despite the jolt of adrenaline. She had prepared for this, but not for the directness of the confrontation, or the absolute certainty in Colette's gaze.

"No more games, Seraphina," Colette said as she sat in the carriage, her gaze sweeping over Seraphina and Aron. "The perfume was a murmur. The snuffbox, a taunt. But this... this grand folly with the duke and your clumsy attempts to implicate me.... You always were too impetuous, too arrogant for your own good. I taught you well, it seems. Almost too well."

Seraphina's chin lifted, a subtle, almost imperceptible tilt, yet it was a defiant challenge. "You taught me to survive, Colette," she stated, her voice steady, betraying none of the shock that had just pierced her. "And to never leave loose ends."

Colette scoffed, a bitter, humourless sound that scraped against the plush silence of the carriage. "Loose ends?" The word was a venomous whisper, then her voice rose, sharp and dangerous, like glass shattering.

"You left me! You vanished from my life, took my money, after 'everything' I did for you!" Her eyes, still burning into Seraphina's, flickered with years of festering resentment, a deep-seated wound now brutally exposed. "And now," she continued, her voice dropping to a low, menacing growl, "you parade as 'Mrs Vance,' a philanthropist, a patron of the arts, building an empire on the very lessons 'I' taught you!"

Colette's gaze hardened, each word a hammer blow. "Now it's time to pay me for what you took. Every last coin you stole, plus interest."

But before Seraphina could formulate a retort, the carriage jolted to a halt. They had arrived back at her home. Just outside, a sudden commotion erupted: the distinctive thud of heavy boots on cobblestones, hushed, urgent voices, and the sharp glint of a lantern beam slicing through the night.

"Bow Street Runners!" Aron hissed, his calm façade cracking as he instinctively peered out the window. His gaze snapped to Seraphina's, alarm plain in his eyes. It was Garrick. The realisation hit Seraphina like a physical blow, and her stomach clenched. What did he want? And more importantly, what did he know? One thing was immediately clear: they had to present a united front.

Colette's eyes widened, a flicker of genuine surprise momentarily eclipsing the white-hot inferno of her rage. She glanced almost imperceptibly at the muffled commotion now growing steadily outside, then back at Seraphina, a predator assessing its cornered prey. The fury in her gaze remained, a constant, burning ember, but a stark, calculating practicality now joined it, cold and sharp as newly forged steel. The game had just changed.

"Looks like your time is up, my darling Seraphina," Colette murmured, her voice barely audible above the rising clamour from beyond the door. Her mind was already racing, assessing the immediate threat, weighing escape routes, calculating probabilities. Her eyes narrowed, fixing on Seraphina with a chilling certainty, a knowing glint. "Maybe your little Eliza has sung like a bird? You always were too sentimental for your own good. It will be your downfall." Her words, delivered with a detached, almost clinical cruelty, were a chilling confirmation, a final, brutal push into the chasm of Eliza's unintentional betrayal.

Seraphina's jaw tightened, a muscle jumping violently in her temple, a solitary tremor betraying her carefully constructed composure. Eliza. The name flashed through her mind, sharp and cold as a freshly honed blade. Had she underestimated the girl's fear, underrated Garrick's ruthless cunning? The weight of her oversight pressed down, a bitter, acrid taste on her tongue. The carefully laid plans, the months of meticulous construction, were now unravelling, hastened by the very piece she had deemed most insignificant. The trap had sprung, but she too was falling into its cruel jaws.

"This is your making, Colette," Seraphina spat, the accusation laced with a raw desperation. But her eyes, locking with Colette's across the cramped carriage, held a plea, stark and undeniable. "He's here for all of us. He'll link this swindle to your presence, to your known methods, and then to me. We are both compromised."

As the driver, urged by Aron, steered the carriage with a jarring lurch towards the back entrance, the three disembarked, hurrying into the deceptive sanctuary of Seraphina's house.

Inside, Colette's gaze, sharp and predatory, swept across the room, taking in the chaotic tableau. Her eyes fell upon the "masterpiece" on the easel, a half-finished canvas gleaming innocently under the gaslight, a testament to Seraphina's audacious fakery. Then, her eyes darted to the frantic dance of lantern beams flickering outside, painting ghostly patterns on the drawn curtains, a clear indication of Garrick's imminent arrival.

Her gaze continued its rapid assessment, cataloguing the instruments of Seraphina's downfall: the meticulously crafted, yet still-drying, "antique" maps, spread carelessly on a side table; the collection of seemingly innocuous "historical relics" — a tarnished chalice, a faux-Roman bust — scattered haphazardly, each a potential thread for Garrick to pull. Lady Montrose's jewels, stolen from a tea party, sparkled still in her mental inventory – they were the very reason Garrick had likely redoubled his efforts, the fresh scent of Seraphina's trail drawing him ever closer.

Aron and Eliza, pale with terror, scrambled to hide the incriminating evidence, sweeping maps into drawers, tossing jewels into velvet pouches, their movements jerky and desperate. But it was too late,

Colette knew. The scent of their panic hung heavy in the air, a testament to their amateurish attempts to erase a crime scene.

The opportunity to reclaim her lost funds from Seraphina had to wait, a sweet, burning desire, a delicious prospect of vengeance she would savour another day. Prison and Garrick could wait. Colette Delacroix, her mind cold and calculating as ever, was already charting an alternative course, one that ensured her freedom, even if it meant leaving Seraphina to face the consequences alone.

As a grim, unwilling understanding passed between the two women, a fragile bridge built over an abyss of betrayal and simmering resentment, a flicker of something akin to shared desperation ignited between them. The venom of their rivalry remained, a raw, burning ember deep within, yet the immediate, pressing threat of Garrick's relentless pursuit forced a temporary, precarious truce. For now, survival superseded vengeance. As a common enemy united them, their individual fates inextricably linked to the frantic dance of lantern beams outside.

The chessboard had been upended. Now, Seraphina and Colette, once mentor and protégé, now bitter enemies, found themselves in the uncomfortable embrace of reluctant allies. Their very survival hinged on the unpredictable intentions of Thomas Garrick. What did he truly know? What did he truly seek? Was he only after the duke's swindle, or had Eliza truly told him of Seraphina's intricate web of deceptions? The silent war between them had exploded into a desperate flight, where mutual destruction was the only alternative to an unholy, temporary alliance against an undeniably formidable adversary.

A Façade of Innocence

The thud of approaching footsteps and the sharp rap on the door echoed ominously through Seraphina's elegant Covent Garden home. But by then, the chaos of moments prior had been meticulously erased. Seraphina Vance and Colette Delacroix, a breath ago locked in a venomous confrontation, now stood side-by-side in the drawing-room, the picture of serene domesticity. Aron, ever efficient, had vanished into the shadows of the house, ensuring no trace of their recent outing remained.

Seraphina's heart still hammered a frantic rhythm against her ribs, but her smile was flawless as the butler announced Garrick's arrival. The frantic dash from the duke's residence, the whispered, furious tactical decisions made in the darkened carriage back to her home – it had been a blur of desperate improvisation. Colette, driven by the immediate threat of imprisonment, had moved with a chilling efficiency that matched Seraphina's own.

"Mr Garrick," Seraphina greeted, extending a graceful hand, her voice warm, laced with a hint of sleepy surprise. "To what do we owe this unexpected, albeit rather late, visit?" She gestured to the untouched teacups on the table, as if they had just settled down for a quiet evening.

Garrick stepped into the room, his eyes sharp, sweeping every corner, every shadow, searching for any sign of evidence, any tell-tale disarray. He took in Seraphina's impeccable gown, Colette's composed presence beside her, and the overall air of undisturbed calm. His frustration was a palpable force.

"My apologies, Mrs Vance," Garrick replied, his voice curt. His fury grew as the scent of his quarry grew cold. "We received information that led us to believe... you might have been in the vicinity of a rather unfortunate incident at the Duke of Rutland's residence earlier this evening. He has had several items of great value stolen."

Seraphina's eyebrows arched in an exquisite pantomime of surprise, her voice a delicate trill. "The Duke of Rutland? Goodness me! My dear man," she began, a hand fluttering to her chest as if genuinely startled, "W have been at home all evening. Enjoying a quiet, perfectly delightful conversation with my dear friend, Madame Delacroix, who you know has only recently arrived from Paris." She paused, a conspiratorial glint in her eyes.

"I'm sure I won't bore you with our utterly enthralling discussions about the latest developments in French fashion, which, as you can imagine, are quite 'lively' these days. Such a frightful scandal, a theft, wasn't it?" Her words, delivered with feigned innocence, were a subtle jab, subtly acknowledging the duke's recent misfortune while maintaining a facade of blissful ignorance regarding its specifics, carefully cultivating the illusion of two cultured ladies utterly oblivious to the chaos unfolding around them.

Colette, her face a mask of elegant indifference, offered a small, polite nod. "Indeed, Mr Garrick. London nights are certainly more eventful than Paris, it seems. One must be vigilant." Her eyes, however, held a flicker of amusement that only Seraphina would catch – a silent appreciation for the audacity of the lie.

Garrick's gaze narrowed, lingering on Colette for a moment, recalling the intelligence he had received about her. He had suspected a connection, but here she was, calmly conversing with the very woman he believed was leading London's swindling rings. The sheer brazenness of the two was almost admirable. He pressed a few more questions about their evening, about any visitors, but their answers, though vague on trivial details, were consistently in lockstep. Without a direct link, without solid proof, he couldn't accuse them. He couldn't even prove they'd left the house.

He finally conceded, his jaw tight. "Very well, Mrs Vance. My apologies for the intrusion. Good night, Madame Delacroix." He turned and left, his footsteps heavy with barely suppressed fury. He had been so close, yet they had slipped through his fingers once more.

As the heavy front door thudded shut, severing them from the escalating chaos outside, Seraphina and Colette exchanged a long, silent look. The air crackled with a brittle tension, the fragile truce holding, for now. A ghost of a smile, slow and chilling, curved Colette's lips.

"You haven't lost your touch, my darling," she murmured, her voice a low, dangerous purr. "A narrow escape." Her gaze, however, held a grim, knowing certainty. "But Garrick will not be so easily deterred."

Without another word, a shared, unspoken understanding passing between them, they moved to the plush velvet settee. Aron, already pouring, handed each woman a crystal glass brimming with the rich, dark port. The liquid, usually a comfort, now felt like a fortifying draught against the encroaching storm. They drank, the stiff, burning warmth a stark contrast to the icy dread that coiled in Seraphina's stomach, and the chilling calculation that flickered in Colette's eyes. For now, they were safe — a brief respite before Garrick came calling again...

The Queen's Invitation and Garrick's Frustration

The following morning brought a crisp, official invitation. Delivered by a royal messenger, its wax seal bore the crest of the Queen's sister. It was a summons to a private soirée, an intimate gathering at one of the royal residences. For Seraphina Vance, it was the culmination of months of meticulous social engineering, a testament to her perfectly crafted persona. The ultimate infiltration.

She read the invitation, a triumphant gleam in her eyes. "A private soirée, Aron," she announced, the note of satisfaction apparent in her voice. "Our efforts have paid off. The Queen's sister herself wishes for our company." Aron nodded, his expression realistic. "An additional level of access. But what of Colette?"

Seraphina glanced towards the guest room where Colette now resides, a silent, watchful viper. "She remains under our roof. A necessary inconvenience for now. Garrick will be scrutinising every move, every associate. Our shared predicament makes her proximity safer than her freedom."

Bow street office

Meanwhile, Garrick sat in his office, the Duke of Rutland case file glaring up at him from his desk. His visit to Seraphina's home had been a humiliating failure. The "lost masterpiece" had been formally acquired by the duke, and the elaborate, fabricated provenance, designed to point to Colette, was too expertly crafted to dismiss, yet too insubstantial to act upon.

"She's too clever, Miller," Garrick muttered, running a hand through his hair. "She hides in plain sight, then vanishes like smoke. Every lead points to her, yet crumbles when I press it. He felt infuriated because his superiors were breathing down his neck for a concrete arrest, but Seraphina Vance, this 'Mrs Vance', remained an untouchable phantom.

The more he pursued her, the more frustrated he became; his inability to pin anything on her was growing into a personal obsession.

He pulled out the reports from Tilly, his operative; the crisp pages rustling softly in the quiet of his office. Eliza Beaumont. Her fears, her desperate confessions – that was his only solid lead, a thread he clung to in the labyrinthine world of these elusive criminals. The girl was clearly terrified, a raw nerve exposed. "Keep pressing, Eliza, Tilly," he had instructed, his voice low and firm. "She is our window into the world of Seraphina Vance. Eventually, Seraphina will make a mistake, and we will be waiting."

The game of cat and mouse had become a perilous three-way dance, each participant moving to an unheard rhythm. Garrick, increasingly bewildered by his elusive quarry, felt the frustration mount with every dead end.

Seraphina, meanwhile, oblivious to the extent of his knowledge, poised for her grandest infiltration, convinced she was merely steps away from her ultimate triumph. And Colette, a silent, vengeful viper, waited, coiled and ready, for her moment to strike, for the perfect opportunity to reclaim what she believed was hers. All the while, Eliza, the unwitting informant, walked a knife-edge between discovery and escape, her every nervous glance and whispered word a potential detonator in this volatile, intricate scheme.

Chapter 8

The Royal Soirée.

The night of the royal soirée arrived, cloaking London in a velvety darkness that perfectly matched Seraphina's mood – a blend of simmering tension and audacious triumph. She moved through her elegant home, a whirlwind of purpose, while Aron meticulously vetted every detail of their plan. Eliza, looking pale but composed, adjusted the lace on Seraphina's gown, her every movement imbued with a newfound anxiety. The recent events had stripped away the last vestiges of her naïve trust, leaving her acutely aware of the perilous tightrope Seraphina walked. Eliza knew her role for the evening was to be the perfectly demure companion, a quiet, unthreatening presence, but the fear of inadvertently exposing Seraphina – and herself – gnawed at her.

"Remember your instructions, Eliza," Seraphina murmured, her voice calm but firm. "Observe, but do not draw attention. Listen, but do not speak unless spoken to. And under no circumstances are you to engage with Garrick if he makes an appearance." Her eyes held a warning that Eliza understood perfectly.

The royal residence wasn't merely grand; it was a dazzling spectacle, a meticulously choreographed ballet of wealth and power. Liveried footmen, each a study in stoic elegance, seemed to glide rather than walk through the vast, echoing marble halls. Overhead, crystal chandeliers sparkled like captured constellations, their myriad facets scattering light into a thousand dancing prisms. The very air thrummed with the hushed murmur of conversations, a sophisticated symphony punctuated by the distant, ethereal strains of a string quartet.

Into this opulent tableau stepped Seraphina. She moved with innate grace, radiating an aura of effortless charm that seemed to draw all eyes without overtly seeking them. She was greeted warmly, almost deferentially, by the Duchess of Gloucester herself. The Duchess, a woman of impeccable lineage and formidable social standing, didn't merely offer a polite nod; she took Seraphina's arm, her grip surprisingly firm, and led her with a distinct sense of purpose towards the inner circle, towards the dais where the Queen awaited.

Seraphina moved through the glittering crowd with magnetic grace, her conversational gambits precise. She spoke of charitable activities, subtly linking them to her fabricated 'Cavendish' legacy, and eavesdropping intently on the nuanced discussions of court politics and personal alliances. Every interaction was a carefully orchestrated performance, designed to deepen her connections and secure her position within the very heart of the monarchy. She was an inch away from the Queen herself, the ultimate prize in her game of influence...

Colette's Calculated Vengeance

Meanwhile, as Seraphina danced on the very edge of royal favour, basking in the gilded glow of the palace, Colette Delacroix remained at the Covent Garden house. A viper, reluctantly coiled in her enemy's lair, every instinct screaming for escape, for vengeance. Her agreement to stay had been purely, excruciatingly practical: the immediate, chilling threat of Garrick's relentless pursuit outweighed her burning desire for immediate retribution against Seraphina.

Yet, the forced proximity was a torment. The very air she breathed felt poisoned by Seraphina's presence. The daily sight of the empire — an empire built with ruthless efficiency and glittering deceit — erected upon Colette's own stolen knowledge, her very ambition, fuelled a cold, relentless fury. It was a silent, festering wound, deepening with every passing hour. Each polished surface, each expensive curtain, each hushed servant, was a stark reminder of what had been taken, twisting the knife deeper into Colette's simmering resentment. She was biding her time, a predator in a gilded cage, waiting for the opportune moment to strike.

Colette had spent her days in the guest room, ostensibly resting, but in truth, she was meticulously planning. She observed the house's routines, the comings and goings of staff, the subtle interactions between Seraphina and Aron. Her sharp intellect, honed by years in the shadows of Parisian high society, was working relentlessly. She saw Eliza's fear, the girl's trembling hands, the way her eyes darted when Seraphina spoke of 'family secrets.' Colette, knowing Eliza's role as an unwitting informant for Garrick, saw not a threat, but a potential pawn.

Her revenge would not be a crude public humiliation. That would bring Garrick's full force down upon both of them, and Colette valued her freedom above all else. No, her vengeance would be precise, devastating, and entirely personal. She would dismantle Seraphina's life, piece by piece, using Seraphina's methods and her own trusted pawns.

Colette started her revenge by sending discreet, untraceable messages. Not to Garrick, not yet, for the Bow Street runner was merely a blunt instrument. Her targets were Seraphina's newly cultivated social contacts, those she was most eager to impress. She hoped to sow seeds of doubt, not about Seraphina's past, but about the future of her grand charitable schemes. Subtle, perfectly timed rumours about "unsound investments" or "unforeseen complications" within certain philanthropic ventures that Seraphina championed. Nothing overt, nothing that could be directly traced, but enough to create a ripple of unease, to subtly undermine the very foundation of trust Seraphina was so carefully building.

Colette watched Eliza over her time at Seraphina's home, a slow, predatory smile playing on her lips. The girl was a vessel of potential, a pawn caught in Garrick's game, and Colette saw her opening. She wouldn't expose Seraphina directly. Instead, she'd orchestrate a scenario where Eliza, in a desperate bid for survival, would be the one to reveal the deepest, most damaging secrets of "Mrs Vance's" empire to Garrick. As the ruin unfolded, Colette would eventually destroy Seraphina completely and irreversibly, regaining what was owed her. As Seraphina graced the royal soirée with her presence, the initial spark of Colette's vengeful plot had just started to ignite.

The royal soirée, with its dazzling display of wealth and power, was nothing more than a glittering distraction to Thomas Garrick. For him, the true game, the relentless hunt, unfolded in the grimy shadows of London's underworld. His initial frustration with the elusive Seraphina Vance had long since hardened into an unyielding resolve. He knew her kind: the brilliant, audacious ones who wove intricate webs of deceit, who truly believed themselves untouchable. After the bewildering, infuriating evening at Seraphina's opulent home, Garrick had systematically shifted tactics, meticulously pulling on every frayed thread he possessed in the city's dark underbelly. He leaned heavily on his contacts in the smoke-filled gin palaces and the illicit gambling dens, squeezing desperate informants with promises of leniency, following every hushed whisper exchanged in the dank, convoluted alleyways.

His persistence, his almost obsessive dedication, finally bore fruit. A former associate of Seraphina's artist-forger – a petty criminal recently snagged for a minor theft – offered a desperate plea bargain. He spoke of a "lady of ice and velvet" who commissioned "lost masterpieces," her eyes as cold and sharp as the diamonds she wore. Separately, a disgruntled former employee of the Duke of Rutland's estate, seething over unpaid bribes, muttered about several clandestine visits concerning a "secret acquisition" and an overly charming "Mrs Vance" who had handled the delicate, clandestine negotiations.

A promising lead came from an unexpected source: a fence, his face a roadmap of scars and suspicious dealings. He reluctantly admitted to Garrick that a new, highly effective operative was gaining notoriety in London's criminal underworld. "Sharp as a razor, Mr Garrick," the fence rasped, his eyes darting anxiously. "They're linked, this Mrs Vance... Some say she's connected to that Frenchwoman... Delacroix." He leaned in closer, his voice dropping to a conspiratorial whisper. "The word on the street is Mrs Vance has got a hideout down by the docks, a warehouse she uses for her bigger consignments. The kind that needs to disappear quickly and quietly. I heard they're moving a large haul of jewels right now, a haul that matches Lady Montrose's pilfered items exactly. It's moving through the underworld with unprecedented speed and discretion."

The pieces, disparate and seemingly unconnected moments before, clicked into place for Garrick with the satisfying precision of a master lock. Madame Colette Delacroix. The undeniable, chilling connection to Seraphina Vance's household. The "lost masterpiece" destined for the unsuspecting duke. It was all inextricably tied together, forming a sinister tapestry of deception. He now possessed the skeletal framework of a vast, interconnected web of swindles, a criminal enterprise centred unmistakably around Seraphina, with Colette now confirmed as a key, and profoundly dangerous, player. He was no longer just chasing individual thieves; he was hunting a syndicate, a hydra with multiple cunning heads.

This potent new intelligence led Garrick directly to a desolate, fog-shrouded warehouse on the banks of the Thames, a known hub for illicit art storage and the darker dealings of the city. Taking a few men, he decided to lay in wait, his heart pounding a furious rhythm against his ribs. It wasn't with apprehension, but with the grim certainty that he was finally, irrevocably, closing in on Seraphina's territory, on the very heart of her illicit operations.

A Near Miss

Seraphina's day dawned with the serene, almost palpable confidence of a general after a victorious campaign. The duke's payment had cleared, a substantial sum that secured their resources for months, a comforting cushion in the precarious world she inhabited. Colette, a viper in her bosom, was undeniably under her roof, confined and, ostensibly, watched. Yet, a growing disquiet, a faint, unsettling hum, vibrated beneath Seraphina's polished composure whenever her thoughts drifted to the Frenchwoman. Eliza, bless her innocent heart, moved through the house like a pale shadow, subdued but diligently performing her duties, utterly oblivious to the new, intricate layers of danger now unfurling around her.

But Seraphina's senses, honed to a razor's edge by years of dancing on the precipice of discovery, pricked with an almost imperceptible shift in the city's rhythm. A particular hansom cab, its maroon paintwork distinctive, had appeared twice in the street outside her home. A tradesman, ostensibly delivering silks, had lingered a moment too long, his gaze too keen, too calculating. She felt it, a visceral certainty – Garrick's presence, the subtle, crafty tightening of his net. The hunter was drawing closer.

Later that afternoon, a frantic signal from one of Aron's street operatives reached Seraphina, the coded message barely coherent, yet its urgency sliced through the calm like a knife. "Runners seen converging on the Thames docks! Warehouse 17!" The words struck Seraphina like a physical blow. Warehouse 17. It was a secondary storage location, a temporary holding place for sensitive items: a trove of initial sketches for future forgeries, a carefully bound ledger containing coded references to specific art acquisitions, and other damning evidence. It was a calculated risk, a loose end Seraphina had thought safely tucked away, a forgotten knot in her meticulously woven web. But news came that Garrick himself was there, leading the charge. He was not just guessing; he was determined, driven by a scent that had led him straight to her hidden vulnerabilities.

"Aron," Seraphina's voice, usually a silken caress, was now sharp, urgent, cutting through the sudden stillness of the drawing-room. "The docks. Warehouse 17. Now." They moved with a synchronised efficiency born of long practice, their actions economical, precise. Seraphina, abandoning all pretence of ladylike gentility, tore off her restrictive stays, pulling on practical, dark clothing, her movements a blur of controlled urgency. Aron was already securing the fastest carriage from the mews. As they sped towards the docks, the wheels clattering furiously on the cobblestones, Seraphina's mind raced, a whirlwind of analytical thought. Garrick would find incriminating evidence there, enough to unravel months of careful work, years even, and Seraphina was not about to let that happen.

They arrived just as the imposing doors of the warehouse shuddered, Garrick's men breaching its flimsy defences. Seraphina reacted instantly, her cunning shining through the immediate danger like a beacon. "Aron," she commanded, her voice low but clear, "the market. A diversion." Aron melted away, a shadow among shadows. A moment later, a sudden, acrid cloud of smoke billowed from a nearby market stall, followed by a chorus of panicked shouts and the thunderous beat of a stampede as merchants and shoppers scattered.

Then, with an audacity that bordered on madness, Seraphina herself made her move. From a concealed pouch, she flung a handful of forged banknotes into the path of the advancing Runners, each note clearly marked with a minor, easily overlooked flaw, yet convincing enough to catch the eye. "Thief!" she shrieked, her voice shrill, deliberately untrained, designed to pierce the din. "They're stealing the Queen's charity funds!"

The Bow Street Runners, momentarily disoriented by the sudden, acrid cloud of smoke billowing from the market and the shrill cries of *"Thief! They're stealing the Queen's charity funds!"* hesitated. Their attention, previously razor-focused on the warehouse, splintered. That fleeting window, a mere breath in the burgeoning chaos, was all Seraphina needed.

With Aron now at her side, a silent, efficient shadow, she didn't flee into the alleys. Instead, they plunged directly *into* the warehouse, not as fugitives, but as architects of a desperate, audacious salvage. A small, well-drilled team, alerted by a pre-arranged signal from Aron, was already in motion. They worked with terrifying efficiency, each knowing their role. They swept sketches for future forgeries, still damp with charcoal, into oilcloth bags. The incriminating ledger, its coded entries a damning testament to Seraphina's illicit empire, vanished into a false-bottomed trunk. Small, ornate frames, awaiting their illicit masterpieces, spirited away, replaced by innocuous crates of imported textiles.

They moved like ghosts, their movements efficient and silent amidst the growing clamour outside. And just as Garrick's heavy boots finally thudded across the threshold, Seraphina and her team were already dissolving into the maze of back alleys, leaving behind a warehouse that, to the untrained eye, was nothing more than a dusty, legitimate storage space. The gamble had been enormous, but who had given Garrick a tipoff? She had risked exposure coming here, but it was to save a critical cache of evidence, and the gamble had worked.

They had escaped, the wind a cold caress on Seraphina's face as they vanished into the labyrinthine streets. But a chilling certainty settled in:

Garrick had an informant. Was it Colette? Eliza? Or someone else entirely? Seraphina knew Garrick would pursue her with renewed, ruthless vigour. The game hadn't just escalated; it had become brutally personal.

Colette's Internal Conflict

Back at the Covent Garden house, Colette Delacroix had witnessed the sudden flurry of activity: Aron's hurried departure, Seraphina's almost desperate urgency, the knowing glance they exchanged. She pieced it together. Garrick was closing in.

As she paced the guest room, the weight of her long-held vengeance felt strangely heavy. She had spent years dreaming of Seraphina's downfall, of reclaiming what was 'hers.' But watching Seraphina react to the immediate threat, seeing the cold brilliance, the daring improvisation that had saved them both from Garrick a few nights before, stirred something unexpected within Colette. A grudging admiration. A spark of pride in her protégé.

She remembered the young Sylvie, so eager, so talented, a reflection of her own younger self. The anger was still there, the deep-seated resentment for the betrayal. Yet, the thought of Seraphina, her brilliant creation, truly imprisoned or destroyed by Garrick's blunt justice, felt… wrong. It wasn't the revenge Colette truly craved. Colette wanted to dismantle Seraphina, to reclaim what she felt was owed, but she wanted

168

Seraphina to witness her own downfall, to suffer the humiliation, not to be destroyed by an outsider. Garrick's victory would be Colette's loss.

The thought, sharp as a diamond cutting glass, struck Colette: if Garrick ensnared Seraphina, Colette's chances of reclaiming her fortune would vanish like smoke. The intricate web of art, influence, and hidden wealth that Seraphina commanded was the very source from which Colette intended to extract her due. A captured Seraphina meant a barren well. And yet, an even more intriguing, more *satisfying* prospect presented itself. Seraphina, stripped of her influence and wealth, but *free* — a fallen empress, vulnerable and exposed — might prove to be a far more exquisite canvas for Colette's ultimate vengeance.

The chessboard, it seemed, had shifted once more, the pieces rearranged by the relentless hand of fate. Colette, the master player, whose strategic mind was as sharp as her wit, recognised the profound alteration. Her intensely personal game with Garrick, previously distinct, now intertwined with her meticulously planned game against Seraphina. It created a dangerous, unforeseen alliance, born not of trust, or even respect, but of shared peril and profoundly conflicting objectives. The deep-seated desire for vengeance, that burning ember in her soul, still glowed fiercely. But a strategic pause, a fresh approach, was not just advisable; it was clearly necessary...

The weeks that unfurled after the audacious Duke of Rutland swindle and the harrowing, breathless escape from Garrick's tightening noose were not a period of recovery for Seraphina, but a dizzying, almost vertiginous ascent. The "lost Elizabethan masterpiece," a triumph of forgery and manipulation, had not only secured the duke's fervent, almost childlike gratitude but, through his proud, expansive boasts and the meticulous cultivation of royal rumours, it had elevated Seraphina to an unprecedented, almost mythical echelon within society. The discreet yet undeniably significant invitation to the Queen's private soirée was not an end in itself, but merely the exquisite beginning. Over the ensuing weeks, a veritable cascade of gilt-edged invitations flowed into the unassuming Covent Garden house: exclusive balls at the resplendent Kensington Palace, intimate musical evenings held within the hallowed halls of Windsor Castle, and even, the crowning jewel, a discreet afternoon tea with the Queen herself, a privilege granted to only the most favoured few.

At these glittering, hothouse events, Seraphina, attired in exquisite fabrics from faraway lands, moved with an almost ethereal grace, her presence radiating a captivating charm that was undeniably the hallmark of one born to a life of privilege, a rare and exquisite bloom cultivated specifically to thrive in the intoxicating atmosphere of the inner circle. Seraphina spoke eloquently, her voice a low, melodic purr, of art and aesthetics, of noble charity initiatives, of her unique, carefully fabricated

'Cavendish' legacy, weaving her invented past into the very fabric of royal society with an artist's precision.

Her influence grew exponentially with each perfectly placed word, each subtly steered conversation, each knowing glance exchanged. She was not merely accepted; she was venerated, sought after, a new, luminous star in the firmament of the ton, eclipsing even long-established luminaries.

Aron, ever her silent, watchful shadow, a figure of unwavering loyalty and quiet intensity, provided the meticulous support, managing the complex logistics of her burgeoning social calendar and guarding their perilous secrets with the ferocity of a silent sentinel. He was the anchor in her dizzying ascent; the unseen hand that ensured her delicate dance on the precipice of discovery remained flawless.

Eliza, though present at these dazzling affairs, found little joy in them. Her role was that of the perfectly demure companion, observing the grand spectacle with a meticulously schooled passivity. Each forced smile, each polite nod, was a heavy weight on her soul. She saw the admiration in the eyes of dukes and duchesses, heard the whispers of Seraphina's impeccable character, and a profound weariness settled over her. She was deeper than ever in the deception, with a constant fear gnawing at her. Garrick was still out there, and Eliza knew, with a dreadful certainty, that her terrified confessions to Tilly were steadily feeding the fire that threatened to consume them all. The lavish gowns felt like a straitjacket, the glittering ballrooms a gilded cage.

While Seraphina danced, not merely with royalty, but *among* them, bathed in the incandescent glow of their favour, Colette Delacroix found a grim, almost perverse satisfaction in her self-appointed task. Confined, yes, to the opulent cage of Seraphina's Covent Garden house; yet granted calculated freedoms for her own clandestine movements, Colette turned the vast, sprawling labyrinth of London into her personal chessboard. Garrick, the ever-earnest inspector, and his diligent runners were merely her unwitting pawns. Her burning, deep-seated desire for vengeance against Seraphina paused temporarily, banked like a cold ember, patiently waiting for the opportune moment to ignite into an inferno. For now, the more pressing matter, the immediate strategic imperative, was twofold: protecting her own intricate network and, by a chilling extension, ensuring Seraphina remained free, a valuable asset awaiting Colette's ultimate, calculated dismantling.

And so, Colette began to deal with Garrick, not as an adversary to be crushed head-on, but as a marionette to be expertly manipulated. She spun elaborate illusions, orchestrating a wild, goose-chase that consumed his resources and patience. She meticulously constructed dead ends, leading him down paths that showcased not just her cunning, but a ruthless, almost artistic mastery of misdirection. Each frustrated sigh from the Inspector, each wasted hour of his men's time, brought a thin, almost imperceptible smile to Colette's lips. She was not just evading him; she was playing him, refining her skills for the grand performance, the one that would ultimately strip Seraphina bare.

She meticulously orchestrated a series of small, intriguing art thefts – a minor landscape from a diplomat's home, a decorative vase from a country estate's city townhouse – each leaving behind tantalising, yet ultimately misleading, clues. A dropped French calling card with a false address. A carefully placed, subtle scent of a specific, rare Parisian tobacco favoured by a notoriously elusive smuggler Colette knew was currently in Calais. A whisper, planted through a low-level informant, about a new, highly organised syndicate operating out of the East End, dealing in stolen silks and jewels, with vague, untraceable links to 'Continental contacts.' Each lead consuming Garrick's time, manpower, and resources. She created elaborate paper trails for phantom art buyers, orchestrated fake meetings at deserted warehouses, and even fabricated a 'confession' from a desperate pickpocket that implicated a shadowy 'French gang' in a dozen unrelated petty crimes.

Garrick, receiving these reports, found himself increasingly exasperated. The leads were many, promising, yet consistently led to nothing. He chased shadows, his men exhausted by fruitless surveillance and frustrated by the lack of concrete evidence. He felt Seraphina Vance slipping further away, disappearing into the untouchable aura of royal favour, even as his instincts screamed her guilt. The constant dead ends, the sheer volume of misinformation, left him fuming. He was certain he was being played, but by whom? He knew Colette Delacroix was in London, potentially collaborating with Seraphina, but her direct involvement in these diversions was maddeningly elusive.

Colette, a silent, predatory observer, watched Garrick's mounting frustration from the safe, luxurious remove of Seraphina's library. Her network of informants, like whispers carried on the wind, reported back to her daily, detailing every misstep, every fruitless pursuit Garrick embarked upon. A faint, almost imperceptible smile, sharp and knowing, played on Colette's lips as she savoured every moment of his escalating discomfiture. She was protecting Seraphina, yes, but this was no act of benevolence. It was a meticulous preservation, ensuring her rival remained intact, vibrant, and powerful – a prize worthy of Colette's ultimate vengeance. She was buying time, not merely for herself, but for Seraphina's empire to burgeon, to grow richer, grander, more influential. The higher Seraphina ascended, the more satisfying would be her eventual downfall. The dance with Garrick, this elaborate game of cat and mouse, was merely a prelude, a warm-up act before the true, ultimate confrontation with her once-beloved, now utterly treacherous apprentice.

The Ultimate Prize: A Daring Proposition

The murmurs of royal favour had grown into a thunderous acclaim for Seraphina Vance. Nobles toasted her name, and the Queen's sister had

174

declared her "a paragon of discernment." But inside Seraphina's opulent study, beneath crystal chandeliers and velvet drapes, a plan was taking shape—one so audacious it bordered on lunacy.

"We're taking the Queen's Jewels," Seraphina said, her voice a low, daring whisper as she stood over a blueprint of St. James's Palace. Her finger traced a path through the layers of security. "Not for riches, Aron. For the thrill. For the legacy."

Aron remained silent, his calculating gaze and raised brow a clear warning. This wasn't a heist; it was a brazen declaration of war against the monarchy itself. The Crown Jewels were a fabled target, guarded by centuries of reverence and steel.

Seraphina's eyes gleamed with an audacious fire. "This will be our magnum opus, a ballet of deception. We'll dance through ghosts and guards. And when it's done, they'll whisper our names like legends."

By the fire, Colette sat poised, reading a book. The uneasy ally, the living reminder of past betrayals—and the one person who had been giving Garrick the runaround.

"And you, Colette," Seraphina said, her voice laced with an ultimate challenge, "you who taught me the very art of the impossible. Do you believe it can be done?"

Colette slowly lowered her book, her eyes, sharp and intelligent, meeting Seraphina's. The cold fury for past betrayals was still there, a thin layer beneath a newfound, pragmatic respect. Seraphina's rise had been spectacular, her sheer audacity captivating. And Colette, recognising the strategic brilliance of such an undertaking, saw an opportunity not just to destroy Seraphina, but to do so after a legendary score they achieved together. It was a twisted form of collaboration, where mutual success would only heighten the eventual bitter fall.

"The jewels are heavily guarded, Sylvie," Colette drawled, deliberately using Seraphina's old name—a blade wrapped in velvet, meant to cut. "But security is just a dance of habit. Find the rhythm, break the pattern, and the whole thing crumbles." A glint of ice flickered in her smile— calculating, amused. "With the right finesse, it's entirely possible."

Thus, the trio was forged: Seraphina, the architect of audacity; Colette, the shadow strategist with venom in her charm; and Aron, the quiet enforcer whose precision made him indispensable. Together, they began to weave a plan not just to steal the Crown Jewels—but to rewrite the rules of impossibility.

Their objective transcended mere gems; it was the ultimate symbol of national power. The elaborate scheme involved fabricating court documents, while subtly influencing palace personnel, and orchestrating a major diversion during a prominent royal function.

Aron brought in his most reliable operatives: a small crew of elusive figures renowned for their distinct talents – picking any lock, moving unheard, and seamlessly disappearing into the urban sprawl. Every minute, every action, every potential problem was meticulously anticipated and planned…

Garrick's Exhaustion and Eliza's Dreadful Discovery

While the queens of deception prepared their ultimate play, Thomas Garrick found himself trapped in a maddening labyrinth of false leads. Colette Delacroix, from within Seraphina's very home, continued to dance him around London. He chased phantom smugglers to deserted docks, raided empty warehouses based on whispered tips, and interrogated minor criminals who offered only convoluted, contradictory tales. His frustration mounted, his superiors' patience wore thin, and the 'Mrs Vance' case seemed to sink deeper into the impenetrable fog of high society.

"They're playing us, Miller," Garrick snarled, slamming his fist onto the desk, scattering half-read reports and redacted dossiers. "They're laughing while we chase shadows." His voice was low, dangerous—coiled with fury. The thefts plaguing the Ton had Seraphina and Colette's fingerprints all over them, he was certain. But every lead dissolved into smoke. Every witness recanted. Every trail ended in silence. He leaned over the desk, eyes burning. "They're ghosts in silk gloves. And I'm done being made a fool." Exhaustion clung to him like a second skin, but beneath it simmered something sharper: obsession. He wouldn't stop until he tore the mask from Seraphina's face—and exposed whatever game she was playing...

Seraphina's house

Meanwhile, a tremor of unease ran through Eliza Beaumont at Seraphina's house; she had sensed a fundamental shift in the air over the past few days. A sharp, almost predatory energy now vibrated beneath Seraphina's polished composure. Eliza's awareness sharpened to the hushed, clandestine meetings that stretched into the late hours in the study, the sprawling palace blueprints unfurled like battle maps, and the chilling, almost devotional way Seraphina uttered "unassailable targets." And then there were Aron's henchmen – their presence grew more frequent, their rough edges and menacing stares a stark contrast to the familiar staff, steadily eroding Eliza's sense of security.

One fateful evening, tasked with fetching a ledger from the study, Eliza saw it. A crumpled sketch discarded beneath the desk. It was crudely rendered, but its subject was terrifyingly clear: the Imperial State Crown, diagrammed with arrows indicating what appeared to be critical vulnerabilities in its display. Below, a terse, scrawled command: "North Chamber - Guard Rotation. Midnight."

An arctic wave of dread, more profound and terrifying than anything she had ever known, enveloped Eliza. This was no mere grift for money. This was an act of breathtaking audacity, a direct, unimaginable assault on the foundational symbols of the Crown. Though the full horror remained just beyond her grasp, the sheer implications were staggering. She had stumbled not just upon a secret, but upon a horrifying truth: Seraphina Vance and her conspirators were planning something catastrophic. The understanding slammed into her, transforming her vague anxieties into a petrifying certainty: she was inextricably caught in a criminal enterprise of monumental scale. The gilded comforts of her life had become a gold-plated cage, and the bars were tightening, threatening to crush her...

Chapter 9

The Ultimate Betrayal

The crumpled sketch of the *Imperial State Crown*, adorned with its chilling annotations, burned itself into Eliza Beaumont's mind. The "lost masterpiece," forgeries and the Duke of Rutland's folly were mere child's play compared to this. Stealing the Queen's Jewels. The sheer, breathtaking audacity of the plan stole Eliza's breath and shattered the last vestiges of her comfortable complicity. She could no longer pretend ignorance, nor could she simply stand by while such a monstrous crime was meticulously orchestrated. The gallows, once a distant, abstract fear, now loomed with terrifying immediacy, a concrete threat to her very existence. Her life, her soul, depended on a single, desperate act: getting away, leaving, or stopping them.

Her decision solidified with an unbearable, unbearable certainty: she had to tell Tilly. She had to expose Seraphina. It was a terrifying, profound act of betrayal, a knife plunged into the trust she'd once held. Yet, the alternative was a lifetime haunted by silent complicity, a gnawing guilt that would devour her from within, or, far worse, utter and complete ruin at the hands of those who plotted this audacious theft. There was no other path.

The next afternoon, Eliza feigned a sudden headache, excusing herself from Seraphina's plans for a social call. She slipped out, clutching her reticule, her heart a frantic drum against her ribs. She made her way to Hyde Park, the designated meeting spot with Tilly, trying to appear nonchalant, as if merely seeking fresh air. Every shadow seemed to hold a lurking figure, every carriage a potential pursuer.

Unbeknownst to Eliza, her furtive movements had not gone unnoticed. Colette Delacroix, ever the shadow dancer, had grown increasingly suspicious of Eliza. The girl's lingering fear, her nervous glances, her recent quietness – all spoke of a secret kept, a loyalty divided. Colette, ever vigilant, had taken to observing Eliza's movements, a quiet, almost invisible presence in her wake.

Colette watched as Eliza, with an almost frantic urgency, approached a woman sitting on a park bench, her posture discreet but alert. Colette recognised the woman instantly: Tilly, a Bow Street Runner she had encountered during her own cat-and-mouse games with Garrick, though Tilly's identity as an operative was carefully concealed from the public. Colette had merely known her as a persistent and annoyingly observant presence in certain circles.

Colette melted deeper into the foliage, close enough to hear the strained whisper of Eliza's voice. "… the Crown… the palace… it's the Queen's Jewels, Tilly! They're planning to steal them!"

Colette's blood ran cold. The Queen's Jewels. Eliza, the naïve pawn, had stumbled upon the ultimate secret. And she was spilling it to Garrick's operative. In that instant, Colette's shifting allegiances solidified into a terrifying clarity. Her vengeful desire to reclaim her fortune from Seraphina was potent, but a successful heist of the Queen's Jewels was a grander prize, a shared triumph that would leave her with a far richer stake. Eliza's betrayal, if allowed to reach Garrick, would not only destroy Seraphina but also utterly compromise Colette and the unprecedented score they were about to achieve.

Colette watched as Tilly, her face grim with the weight of the confession, questioned Eliza further. The girl was too scared, too desperate. She would tell everything. Colette's mind, a razor-sharp instrument of survival, instantly processed the grim implications. There was no time for subtlety, no room for error. Eliza knew too much, and her testimony would bring down the entire audacious scheme, along with Seraphina, Aron, and, by extension, Colette herself.

A cold, ruthless resolve settled over Colette. There was only one way to ensure the plan's success, and her own safety. Eliza Beaumont had to be silenced. Permanently. The quiet girl, who had longed for a comfortable, simple life, had just signed her own death warrant, not with a pen, but with a desperate whisper in Hyde Park.

The Serpent Strike

The chill that ran through Colette as she watched Eliza confide in Tilly in Hyde Park solidified into a cold, lethal resolve. The Queen's Jewels. The ultimate score. Eliza's desperate whisper threatened to unravel everything, to drag them all into the inescapable net of Garrick's justice. There was no other choice. Seraphina's entire future, their shared ambition, depended on the silencing of this one, frightened girl. And beneath Colette's calculated ruthlessness simmered a deeper, more possessive motive: she would eliminate any threat to Seraphina, even those Seraphina herself held dearly.

So that evening, during their evening meal, Colette moved with practiced stealth. A tiny, almost imperceptible pinch of dark, dried herb, pulverised to a fine powder, slipped from Colette's palm into the steaming cup as she passed it to Eliza. It was a poison known only to a select few in the Parisian underworld, undetectable to the common physician, designed to mimic a wasting illness, a gradual fading of life.

The next day, Eliza complained of a mild fever and a persistent cough. Seraphina, concerned, insisted she rest, believing it a common chill caught in the damp London air. But over the following days, Eliza's condition steadily worsened. Her once bright eyes became dull, shadowed with an increasing lethargy. Her appetite vanished, her cough became a dry, rattling gasp, and a subtle pallor settled over her skin. She became weaker, her movements slow and arduous.

Seraphina and Aron were distraught. They summoned the most reputable physicians in London, who examined Eliza with grave faces, muttering about "consumption" and "a wasting sickness," but offering no cure, only tonics that did little to stem the tide. Colette, ever present, watched Eliza's decline with an almost detached interest, offering soothing words and comforting brews – brews that sometimes, unbeknownst to anyone, contained another, infinitesimally small dose of the undetectable herb, ensuring the poison's relentless work. She played the concerned companion flawlessly, her outward composure masking the grim satisfaction within. "Such a delicate flower," she would sigh to Seraphina, her eyes filled with feigned sorrow. "London's fogs are cruel to those not accustomed to its rigours."

During the days leading up to Colette's quiet act of murder, Eliza Beaumont underwent a noticeable transformation, as her once-bright eyes lost their lustre, her laughter disappeared and was replaced by silence, and her steps became increasingly unsteady. Lost in thought, she would sit for hours on end, staring out the frost-laced windows while murmuring fragments of secrets that were far too heavy for her failing body to carry any longer. "The Crown... the palace... Garrick knows..." But her voice was thin, her words scattered like leaves in the wind, and those around her dismissed them as fevered nonsense.

Seraphina stayed close, her concern genuine, her grief mounting with each passing day. She brushed Eliza's hair, read to her from old novels, held her hand through the long, sleepless nights. She never suspected that the girl she had once protected was now slipping away by design. Colette watched from the shadows, her expression unreadable, her heart a battlefield of triumph and torment.

On a cold, grey morning, a week after the poison first touched Eliza's lips, the girl exhaled her final breath—a shallow whisper that barely stirred the air. Her death was quiet, almost polite, as if she didn't want to trouble anyone. Seraphina wept openly, cradling Eliza's lifeless body with a sorrow that cut deep. She had loved her, in her way. And now she was gone.

Aron, ever the stoic, handled the burial with quiet efficiency. A modest grave, a simple headstone, no questions asked. The physicians had no answers. The illness had no name. And Colette, ever meticulous, had left no trace.

But in the silence that followed, something lingered. A tension. A shadow. Eliza's final murmurs haunted Seraphina's dreams. And though no one suspected foul play, the truth had not died with Eliza— it had merely gone underground, waiting for the right moment to rise.

Colette's Triumph and Twisted Affection

While Seraphina was overcome with grief, Colette remained distant and detached from the situation, experiencing a disturbing feeling of triumph that took hold of her. The threat vanished, and the grand heist of the Queen's Jewels could continue, unburdened by Eliza's terrified confessions. Her vengeance against Seraphina, for now, had yielded to a more pressing, and far more intimate, desire.

Colette watched Seraphina, her heart a twisted knot of possessive love and raw, burning ambition. She had moulded Seraphina, sculpted her into the magnificent, brilliant woman she was today. Seraphina was not merely her protégé; she was the culmination of Colette's genius, her most exquisite creation. It was a deep, burning, romantic love, fiercely possessive and utterly unyielding. Every spark of Seraphina's wit, every daring gamble, ignited a passion within Colette that transcended their criminal enterprise.

A simmering, quiet jealousy consumed Colette as she watched the effortless bond between Seraphina and Aron. To Colette, he was a rival, a barrier to having Seraphina all to herself. Colette was patient. Eliza had been the first obstacle, and Aron would follow when the moment was right. She could wait until Seraphina's empire had amassed enough wealth to be ripe for the taking.

"Soon, *ma chérie*," Colette mused, her eyes locked on Seraphina's bowed head, the delicate tremble in her shoulders as grief rippled through her. "Soon, you'll see it clearly. The others—they coddle you, misunderstand you, dilute your brilliance with sentiment and softness. But I... I see you." Her thoughts curled like smoke, dark and intoxicating. "I see the hunger behind your elegance, the fire beneath your poise. And I alone have the strength to match it. To shape the world, you deserve. To burn away the weak and the foolish who would hold you back."

She watched Seraphina cradle Eliza's memory with trembling hands and felt no guilt. Only certainty. You will come to me. Not out of love, not at first. But out of necessity. Out of truth. And when you do, you'll understand: I am the only one who would do what must be done. For you. For us... Her lips barely moved, but the promise was etched into her soul. *Soon you will be mine. And the world will kneel before us.*

Thomas Garrick, a man whose patience was as thin as the London fog on a winter morning, received the news of Eliza Beaumont's sudden, mysterious death with a chilling sense of dread and seething frustration. His primary informant, the very window into the insidious Vance operations, was gone. Deceased. The physicians' reports, delivered with all the sombre certainty of their profession, spoke of a swift, incurable illness—a common enough pronouncement in the teeming, disease-ridden rookeries and elegant drawing-rooms of this 1800s London. But Garrick felt a cold, hard knot of suspicion tightening in his gut. It was too convenient. Too neat. Too damned perfect.

"Consumption, they say, Miller," Garrick practically spat, tossing the flimsy medical report onto his cluttered desk, its surface strewn with half-eaten biscuits and dog-eared case files.

"Convenient, isn't it? Just when Miss Beaumont was proving useful." He rubbed a hand over his weary eyes, the gaslight casting long, dancing shadows across his face. He knew, with an instinct honed by years on the city's grimy streets, that something was profoundly wrong. He couldn't prove foul play; the symptoms, so vaguely described, painted a picture of an illness that swept through the city with terrifying regularity.

Yet, the timing, following Eliza's terrified, breathless confessions about the Queen's Jewels plot, screamed of something far more sinister. He was utterly, absolutely certain that Seraphina Vance, or some shadowy hand connected to her, was responsible. But without a body to autopsy—and good luck securing one in this labyrinthine legal landscape for a death deemed "natural"—without a single trace of poison to be found, he was utterly, agonisingly helpless.

The death of Eliza, however, hardened Garrick's resolve like tempered steel. It stripped away any lingering doubts about Seraphina Vance. He felt with chilling clarity that she was capable of anything, including cold-blooded murder to protect her secrets.

The investigation into the plot to steal the Queen's Jewels, still nebulous but growing clearer with each revelation, gained a terrifying, visceral urgency. Garrick knew he was up against a formidable, ruthless opponent, one who would stop at nothing to achieve her aims and bury anyone, no matter how insignificant, who dared to stand in her way. He was in a fight for more than justice; he was in a fight for the very soul of the city, against a darkness that promised to consume them all.

Chapter 10

The Viper Uncoils

The elegant house on the fringe of Covent Garden, once a sanctuary for secrets, now resonated with a chilling new kind of dread. Scarcely days had passed since Eliza's quiet burial when a disturbingly familiar affliction manifested. Aron, almost imperceptibly at first, mirrored Eliza's inexplicable symptoms: a lingering cough, a creeping disinterest in food, and a pallor that deepened with each passing day. Seraphina, her heart still aching from Eliza's loss, felt an icy knot of premonition tighten within her. The precision was unnerving; the familiarity, terrifying.

Her mind, a finely calibrated instrument of perception and logic, began assembling disparate pieces she had previously dismissed as harmless. Colette's subtle yet persistent habit of preparing Aron's morning tea. The tender solicitude with which she would proffer a specific tonic. The quiet, almost imperceptible gleam of satisfaction in Colette's eyes—a glint Seraphina had tragically mistaken for the balm of mutual sorrow. Then, a long-dormant memory surged forward: Colette's almost obsessive interest in toxicology during Seraphina's early training, particularly her detailed lessons on rare, undetectable botanical agents designed to perfectly imitate natural illness. The horrifying truth struck Seraphina with the force of a physical impact: Eliza had not succumbed to fate. She had been deliberately killed. And Aron was marked to follow.

Seraphina's grief for Eliza curdled into a scorching, white-hot rage. How could she have been so naïve, so absorbed in her ambitions that she failed to see the viper living in her home?

She wouldn't confront Colette directly. Instead, Seraphina moved with a chilling precision born of fury and fear. She began subtly intercepting Aron's prepared drinks, replacing them herself, meticulously searching for the familiar, earthy bitterness that had likely poisoned Eliza. Her gaze, sharp and analytical, now tracked Colette's every movement and expression, seeking the telltale signs of a predator.

Days bled into a torturous week as Seraphina meticulously shadowed Colette, her senses strained, her every nerve alight with a terrible suspicion. Then, after what felt like an eternity of agonising scrutiny, she found it. Tucked away beneath a cleverly disguised loose floorboard in Colette's guest room, nestled within the shadowed dust, was a tiny, exquisitely crafted wooden box.

Her heart pounding, Seraphina opened it. Amidst withered blossoms and brittle, faded letters, lay a small, tightly sealed glass vial. Inside, a tiny quantity of dried, dark powder. She brought it closer, and the faint, almost imperceptible aroma rose—an acrid, earthy scent that pierced through her dread with chilling recognition. It was precisely what Colette, with a disturbing academic relish, had detailed years ago: *Atropa belladonna,* deadly nightshade. The very herb whose slow, insidious poison flawlessly mimicked consumption. The same botanical agent

Seraphina believed Colette had used to create the perfect, undetectable murder.

With the vial clutched, a cold, hard truth in her palm, Seraphina stalked Colette to the elegant drawing-room. Her voice, when she spoke, was a silken trap, belying the volcanic rage churning beneath. Upstairs, Aron drifted into a fragile sleep, utterly unaware of the deadly drama unfolding.

"The Atropa Belladonna, Colette," Seraphina began, her hand raising, allowing the light to glint off the dark powder within the glass. "A specific choice. Yet so terribly effective, wasn't it? Eliza's farewell was… remarkably serene."

The intricate mask Colette wore, usually so impenetrable, shattered. Her eyes, typically calm as glass, flared with a fleeting horror, then hardened into glinting shards of pure, unadulterated venom. "So, the student recalls her tutelage, Sylvie," she whispered, her voice a low purr as she rose, every movement imbued with a terrifying, predatory elegance. "A shame the curriculum was incomplete. Eliza was merely a loose end, a simpering informant. A weakness you lacked the resolve to sever, so I performed the necessary surgery. For you. For us."

"For us?" Seraphina's voice splintered, a fragile dam struggling against a tidal wave of fury. "You extinguished an innocent life! For what— nothing! And now you dare to turn your depravity upon my Aron!

Don't you dare deny it; I have witnessed the identical torment in him, but he is fighting back! My Aron! My very partner! My family!"

"Family? That weak man is a chain, Sylvie, a hindrance holding you captive," Colette's voice, a low and dangerous rumble, slithered across the room, wrapping Seraphina in a chill of dread. "He doesn't deserve you. I do. I would lay the world at your feet. I would tear down every single thing that stands in our way."

Colette's gaze burned with an obsessive fire, her words a desperate plea. "Can't you see, ma chérie? I adore you. It's a passion that burns hotter than any family bond, a love that eclipses any other partnership. I will protect you. I will set you free." Her voice dropped to a raw, breathless whisper. "Can't you see I love you? Leave this wreck of a man. Run away with me. Be mine, irrevocably mine."

Her words, twisted with a chilling possessiveness, only fuelled Seraphina's rage. "You are quite mad, Colette!"

As Seraphina lunged forward, not for a blow, but to grasp Colette, to force her to face the horror of her confession, Colette moved with the speed of a serpent. She ducked, sidestepped, her hand flashing to a hidden knife sheath at her ankle. "A pity, then," Colette hissed, her eyes blazing with a mixture of thwarted love and renewed hatred. "You always were too sentimental. I will take the Queen's Jewels alone, then.

And you can explain to Garrick why your partner lies dying of 'consumption' beside a murdered informant."

With a sudden, brutal motion, Colette lunged forward and shoved Seraphina hard, sending her reeling. Her heels scraped against the polished floor as she staggered back, colliding with the edge of a settee. Before Seraphina could regain her footing, Colette was already moving—vaulting over the furniture with feline grace, flinging open the drawing-room doors so violently they ricocheted off the walls. A blur of black silk and fury, she vanished down the corridor.

Seraphina scrambled upright, breath caught in her throat, just in time to hear the front door slam with finality. A moment later, the distant clatter of carriage wheels echoed through the morning fog, fading into silence.

Colette Delacroix was gone. But the audacious plan to steal the Queen's jewels was still in motion. Colette, driven by her monstrous ambition and now a desperate need to escape, intended to carry it out herself, even without Seraphina or Aron. The ultimate prize, now the ultimate weapon, hung in the balance, dangling between a vengeful former mentor, a betrayed master swindler, and a relentless Bow Street Runner, unaware that the game had just taken a terrifying turn for the worst.

As the front door slammed with a sound akin to a gunshot, Seraphina was left not only with the lingering sound of Colette's unsettling exit but also with the painful aftermath of her horrifying admission. The room felt scorched by it, as if the very air recoiled.

Aron was upstairs, in a helpless state, as his body was being ravaged by the very same poison that had taken Eliza's life. Although Seraphina was unaware of the exact amount he had taken, the doubt surrounding the situation served only to intensify her anger. As of that moment, she understood that Eliza's death was not because of an illness of any kind. The evidence suggested that she had been murdered. Seraphina's confrontation with Colette prevented Aron from becoming her next target, which would have happened otherwise.

A cold, surgical rage sliced through her shock. Colette's twisted declaration of love—her claim that everything had been for Seraphina—was grotesque. It wasn't love; it was a perversion; a violent obsession dressed in velvet. Seraphina's hands trembled, not with fear, but with a new, fierce resolve. Colette had crossed a line that could never be uncrossed.

There was no time to lose. Seraphina's world narrowed to a single, urgent point: Aron. Her mind raced as she tore through her old books, frantically sifting through every detail of Colette's toxicology lessons, searching for an antidote. All the while, she watched Aron—pale and sweating, his breathing terrifyingly shallow. She found the right ingredients and quickly mixed a potent emetic, followed by a series of neutralising herbal concoctions. Forcing them down his throat, she watched as the next few hours became a desperate vigil. He writhed, then slowly, agonisingly, began to stabilise. He was weak, but he would live.

It was Aron's pale, drawn face that solidified Seraphina's next audacious decision. Colette had crossed a line, one from which there was no return. The game had shifted from a contest of wits to a matter of life and death, of justice. There was only one man who could truly stop Colette now, and despite the monumental risk, Seraphina knew she had to face him…

Hours later, as the first pale fingers of dawn stretched across the grimy London skyline, painting the rooftops with a bruised purple, Seraphina Vance stepped into Thomas Garrick's office at Bow Street. She moved with a deliberate, almost spectral calm. Her eyes, though heavily rimmed with red, burned with an unyielding, almost frightening, resolve. In her hand, she clutched a small, tightly sealed leather pouch.

Garrick, still in the disarray of an abrupt summons, looked up from his cluttered desk, a mixture of suspicion, weariness, and profound surprise etched onto his craggy features. He straightened, his chair scraping against the floorboards. "Mrs Vance," he stated, his voice flat, devoid of its usual bluster, betraying a hint of unease. "To what precisely do I owe the... pleasure... of this highly irregular dawn visitation?"

"My dear Mr Garrick," Seraphina began, her voice a low, genuine whisper, trembling with a controlled anguish. "I have just learned of a horror that defies belief. A crime of such magnitude, it threatens the very security of the Crown. And the mastermind, the murderer, is Madame Colette Delacroix."

She moved with a grim purpose, placing a small, elegantly carved wooden box directly onto his desk. The faint clatter seemed to shatter the peace of the room. "My dear Mr Garrick," she stated, her voice tight with suppressed emotion, "this is the very embodiment of her derangement. Contained in this box is the poison that murdered Eliza Beaumont." Her fingers brushed a vial as she added, "And this... this has been systematically used to attempt the slow, painful death of my beloved Aron." She held his gaze, her own burning with a fierce clarity.

"Mr Garrick, both lives were to vanish under the convenient, deceptive guise of 'consumption.' By some cruel twist of fate, or perhaps divine intervention, I recently recalled a very specific lesson from my nursing days—how certain poisons can be countered. Had that knowledge not resurfaced, Aron would be as irrevocably lost to me as Eliza." Her voice snagged, a raw, painful sound. "But, Eliza... I could not save her."

Then Seraphina added. "Colette Delacroix, Mr Garrick," she said, her voice like ice cracking over deep water, "is not only a poisoner and a murderer. She is a thief of staggering audacity. She intends to steal the Queen's jewels." The silence that followed was suffocating.

"She's been orchestrating this for months," Seraphina continued, her gaze drilling into him. "Twisting my access, exploiting my connections, weaving a treasonous plot right under my nose." Garrick stared, his face ashen, the sheer audacity of her words leaving him speechless. He couldn't reconcile the words and actions Seraphina was describing.

"Yes, she's fled," Seraphina said, "but this is no retreat. It's a calculated pivot. She has detailed maps of the North Chamber and knows the guard rotations down to the minute. Her plan hinges on a grand diversion during the upcoming royal gala, timed perfectly. And when I confronted her, she fled." She leaned forward, her voice low and lethal. "This isn't desperation. It's vengeance. And it's imminent."

Garrick stared a moment longer, his mind reeling. The scale of the plot, the cold-blooded murder of Eliza, the poisoning of Aron, the sheer audacity of it all – it was almost too fantastical. He studied Seraphina's face, searching for the tell-tale flicker of deception. She appeared genuinely distraught, terrified, yet also utterly convincing. He recalled Eliza's fears, her information to Tilly, now tragically cut short. The puzzle pieces, once scattered, now clicked into a terrifying picture, all centred on Colette Delacroix.

But Garrick was no fool. His suspicion of Seraphina Vance ran deep. He knew her capacity for deception, her network, her connections. The ease with which she laid blame solely on Colette, portraying herself as a horrified victim, was almost too perfect. He was almost certain she had been involved in the plans from the start, perhaps even the poisoning of Eliza, before Colette turned on her.

Yet, a cold, hard truth presented itself. The very inner circle of the Royal Family held Seraphina, 'Mrs Vance in the highest regard by the Queen's own sister. She was a favoured guest; her status flawless. To arrest her now, without irrefutable proof beyond her own confession, would cause an unimaginable scandal, a diplomatic incident, and political fallout that Garrick, for all his stubborn integrity, could not unleash. The Crown, as always, would protect its darlings.

A grim smile touched Garrick's lips. He had suspected Seraphina for months, chased her through the shadows, and now, here she was, offering him the greatest prize of all: Colette Delacroix, the elusive French criminal, attempting the ultimate heist. And Seraphina, whether truly innocent or merely cornered, was offering the inside track.

"Mrs Vance," Garrick said, his voice slow and measured, "you claim Colette Delacroix is acting alone, that she is the sole architect of this madness. And you have evidence of her murderous intent." He picked up the vial. "Very well, if, as you say, the Crown Jewels are at stake, and given your unique position within the royal circle, your intimate knowledge of this villainess's methods, I require your assistance."

Seraphina's eyes, meeting his, held a complex mix of relief, cold triumph, and a chilling understanding of the bargain they were making. "My assistance, Mr Garrick?"

"Yes," Garrick confirmed, leaning forward, his voice a low, gravelly command. "You will proceed as if nothing has occurred. You will attend the next royal event as planned. We will use the plan she devised, but this time, it will be a trap for her. And you, Mrs Vance, will be the bait."

Seraphina's spine stiffened, a fleeting flicker of apprehension crossing her features, instantly superseded by an unyielding, almost chilling resolve. She was gambling everything—her reputation, her freedom, perhaps even her life—by laying bare Colette's grand design. But she would do it. For Aron, for the innocent memory of Eliza, and for the ruthless preservation of her own meticulously constructed reputation. She would become Garrick's unwitting decoy.

The Queen's jewels would not be stolen. Not yet. Seraphina's true purpose was far more precise: she wanted Colette Delacroix to fall, caught irrevocably in a snare woven by Seraphina herself—the dark pupil, now the master—with the unwitting, potent assistance of the Crown and the very law Colette so arrogantly sought to outwit.

The night of the Queen's ball descended upon London, a dazzling spectacle of light and gaiety, yet within the hushed grandeur of St. James's Palace, a deadly silent drama was poised to unfold. Tonight was the presentation of the younger ladies of the gentry, a prestigious coming-out party where every guest, a symbol of purity and new beginnings, was dressed in resplendent white – a sea of silk, satin, and lace, shimmering under the glow of a thousand candles.

Seraphina Vance, radiant in a gown of ivory brocade that seemed to absorb and reflect every ounce of light, moved through the grand ballroom with a delicate grace. Her face, composed and serene, betrayed nothing of the churning maelstrom within. Grief for Eliza, mingled with a burning cold fury at Colette's monstrous betrayal, warred with her absolute resolve to protect Aron and her hard-won position. She was the bait, the radiant lure in Garrick's elaborate snare.

Aron, still pale and a little frail from the poison, stood discreetly near one of the ballroom's grand entrances, his gaze fixed on Seraphina. He knew his role: to be present, to appear recovered, and to provide the quiet, dependable anchor Seraphina needed. His own face was a mask, hiding the lingering weakness and the profound, silent horror of Colette's true nature.

Garrick, disguised as a visiting country gentleman of considerable means, moved through the fringes of the crowd, his eyes missing nothing. His men, meticulously briefed, were positioned with surgical precision. Some mingled with the footmen, others posed as guards, their gazes sweeping the exits, the corridors, the very air itself for any anomaly. Garrick felt the familiar thrill of the hunt, intensified by the knowledge that the target was a master of her craft, and the stakes were nothing less than the Crown Jewels. The information Seraphina had provided, delivered with a chilling certainty, had made the impossible seem terrifyingly real.

The trap, a perilous modification of Colette's own audacious design, was set around the display of the Regalia of the Young Princesses, a lesser but still incredibly valuable collection of jewels and tiaras traditionally presented during this specific ball, often displayed in the Queen's North Chamber for a short period before being returned to the Tower. Colette's original plan had centred on exploiting a known brief lapse in guard rotation during a specific musical interlude.

That "lapse" in security, once a genuine oversight, was now a meticulously orchestrated void, overseen by Garrick's most trusted men, their positions concealed and precise. The North Chamber itself, seemingly accessible only via the chaotic elegance of the ballroom, was now covertly riddled with a network of concealed bell systems, each acting as a silent alarm, ready to shriek Colette's presence to Garrick's waiting team.

Colette's plan hinged on a dramatic diversion within the ballroom – a calculated chaos designed to draw all eyes, while she made a swift, surgical entry into the Chamber. Seraphina and Garrick had anticipated this with chilling accuracy. Indeed, Garrick himself had subtly facilitated the very minor, pre-determined "lapses" in security that Colette, in her arrogance, would expect and rely upon, drawing her deeper into the precise, inescapable killing zone they had prepared.

Amidst the swirling sea of white gowns, the gentle strains of the orchestra, and the delighted laughter of debutantes, Seraphina held her breath. Her eyes, subtly scanning the faces around her, searched for a hint of Colette. She knew her former mentor would be here. Colette was too proud, too consumed by ambition and her warped desire to prove her superiority, to miss the opportunity for the ultimate score. She would be disguised, of course, a phantom in the crowd, a master of blending in.

Then, Seraphina saw her. A fleeting glimpse of a dark figure, incongruous amidst the white, moving with an unnatural fluidity near a service entrance. Colette Delacroix. Dressed as a servant, her face obscured by a lowered cap, yet Seraphina recognised the subtle arrogance in her posture, the purposeful grace of her movements. She was heading towards the North Chamber.

An icy dread mixed with a grim satisfaction in Seraphina's heart. The bait had been taken. The Queen, unwitting orchestrator of this deadly game, continued to beam from her dais, surrounded by her radiant young ladies. The ball, a magnificent façade of innocence and joy, was about to become the stage for a dramatic reckoning between two former confidantes, played out under the watchful, expectant eye of Thomas Garrick. The Royal Jewels were the prize, but Colette's freedom, and Seraphina's very future, were the true stakes.

The Falcon's Escape and the Queen's Shield

The strains of a waltz still filled the grand ballroom, a mesmerising rhythm that belied the deadly silence unfolding in the North Chamber. Colette Delacroix, a shadow amidst the pristine white, moved with the stealth of a cat burglar. She had timed her infiltration perfectly, slipping into the ornate chamber through a concealed service door during the crescendo of the orchestra. Her movements were fluid, precise, as she headed for the glittering display case containing the Princesses' Regalia. She knew the exact 'lapse' in the guard rotation, a detail provided by Seraphina herself, now a strategically placed void in Garrick's trap.

As Colette's gloved hand reached for the latch on the display case, a sharp, metallic click echoed in the quiet chamber. Alarm bells, previously dormant, rang forth through the palace, cutting through the music of the ball. Footsteps pounded down the corridor. Garrick's trap had sprung.

Colette cursed, a sharp, frustrated hiss escaping her lips as her eyes darted wildly. This was not the smooth, unimpeded entry she had planned. The immediate clamour of unseen bells, a jarring, unwelcome surprise, shattered the silence of the chamber. She spun, a chilling realisation dawning: the 'lapse' was a snare, expertly woven. At that precise moment, Garrick's men burst into the chamber, a wave of grim faces, truncheons drawn and ready.

"Madame Delacroix! Hold!" Garrick's voice boomed, cutting through the tension, his own heavy truncheon pointed directly at her, a silent, blunt accusation.

But Colette was no stranger to desperate escapes. With a burst of frantic energy, she hurled a small, heavy velvet bag – filled with lead weights – directly at Garrick's head. He ducked momentarily disoriented. Colette used the precious seconds not to flee through the main exit but to shatter a tall stained-glass window at the rear of the chamber with a brutal kick. Shards of coloured glass exploded outwards, creating a cacophony that startled the guards. Before they could react, she plunged through the gaping hole, dropping into the rose garden below, a dizzying array of thorns and darkness.

The palace erupted in a frenzy. The blaring alarms shattered the illusion of the ball's tranquillity. Shouts of "Thief!" and "Intruder!" rippled through the hallways, yet, astonishingly, the grand ballroom remained largely insulated. The Queen, engaged in a conversation with a foreign dignitary, merely looked up, a frown creasing her brow at the distant commotion, assuming it to be a minor staff incident.

The music had paused, but the sheer size of the palace and the compartmentalised nature of the events kept most of the royal guests, awash in white, unaware of the full scale of the breach.

Seraphina Vance, ever composed, stood near the Queen's dais. When the alarms first pierced the air, she subtly tensed, her gaze flicking towards the North Chamber's direction. But her years of training instantly took over. She turned, her expression one of polite curiosity, not alarm. As the initial panic settled, she used the moment to her advantage.

"Your Majesty," Seraphina said, her voice clear, resonant, drawing the Queen's attention. "It seems there is some minor disturbance, but for a moment such as this, celebrating the blossoming grace of our young ladies, such trifles should not mar the occasion." She then curtsied deeply, and with a regal flourish, presented a large, exquisitely enamelled chest to the Queen's lady-in-waiting.

"May I present, Your Majesty," Seraphina began, her voice poised and resonant, "a humble token of my enduring admiration for your unwavering dedication to the orphans of London. A donation of five thousand guineas, to be used entirely at your discretion for the Queen's Orphanage."

A collective gasp rippled through the crowd. Five thousand guineas— an astonishing sum. Heads turned, fans fluttered, and whispers of awe spread like wildfire. It was not merely a gift; it was a declaration. A public testament to Seraphina's immense generosity, her influence, and her unshakable grace under pressure.

The Queen, momentarily distracted from the distant echo of alarms, turned her full attention to Seraphina. Her eyes softened, her smile widened. "Mrs Vance!" she exclaimed, stepping forward with regal warmth. "My dear, you are too kind! A true blessing to those less fortunate. Your grace and generosity are truly a credit to our nation."

Then, with a gesture that silenced the murmurs around them, the Queen extended her gloved hand. "You must join me for tea at Buckingham House this Thursday. I insist. There is much I would like to discuss—your vision, your charitable work, your remarkable poise. You are precisely the sort of woman this country needs."

Seraphina curtsied with perfect precision, her heart steady, her mind razor-sharp. The invitation was more than a social honour—it was a shield. In the chaos of Colette's escape, Seraphina had not only preserved her reputation; she had elevated it. The royal family, already holding her in high esteem, now saw her as indispensable. A bastion of benevolence. A symbol of stability.

And for Garrick, watching from the edge of the crowd, the implications were clear. Whatever suspicions he harboured, whatever threads he hoped to pull—Seraphina Vance had just wrapped herself in the most unassailable armour of all: royal favour.

Chapter 11

End Game

Garrick stood amidst the wreckage of his carefully laid trap, his face a mask of barely controlled fury. The shattered window, a gaping wound in the chamber wall, and the scattered disarray spoke volumes of Colette's desperate, last-gasp escape. She had slipped through his fingers, an infuriating ghost, but the bitter taste of that momentary victory would soon curdle for her. He had the mark of the woman now; not a physical one, but a deep, ingrained understanding of her ruthless ambition. He knew with absolute certainty that desperation would consume her to get away, perhaps even flee the country. The discarded lead weights – evidence of her intent to create a decoy for the Queen's Jewels – and the carefully feigned target confirmed her singular, unyielding ambition: to complete the heist, even if she had to do it alone. But why? Why had she risked everything to escape, only to leave such clear signs of her true objective?

His frustration, a coiling snake in his gut, sharpened his commands. "Spread out!" he barked, his voice cutting like a whip. "Search every port, every coach station, every road out of London! She's wounded but not broken. Find her!"

Colette Delacroix vanished, dissolving into the city's murky depths for two gruelling days. The scratchy wools and drab linens of a common woman, a disguise as much for her appearance as for her shattered pride, replaced the silks and satins that had defined her station. She moved like a phantom, her steps hurried and furtive, through London's labyrinthine underbelly – the reeking, cobbled lanes, the suffocating

211

press of the impoverished, the shadowed doorways that promised only fleeting concealment. She was relentless in her desperate bid for freedom, her mind sharp and resourceful even as her body ached with constant vigilance. But the isolation was a crushing weight; every rustle of leaves, every distant shout, every curious glance was a potential noose tightening around her neck. Her desperate hope, her only chance, was to melt away, to become a nameless refugee on the Continent. The opulent life she had clawed her way to was gone, leaving only the bitter taste of destitution and the constant, chilling dread of a woman perpetually on the run from the unforgiving arm of the law.

On the third night, a thick Thames fog, heavy and suffocating, wrapped the deserted wharf. Colette, moving like a hunted animal, crept through the clinging air. Each breath was a struggle, each step a gamble. Her heart hammered against her ribs, a frantic, deafening rhythm trying to outrun the inevitability that stalked her.

Ghostly fingers of fog curled around her, obscuring everything. With wild, red-rimmed eyes, she strained to see the faint outline of her salvation: a small freighter bound for Calais. Somewhere beyond the veil of mist, freedom waited. She could almost taste the salt of the Channel and feel the foreign wind on her face.

Out of the shadows, the captain emerged. His features were indistinct, a blur of suspicion and weariness. Colette had arranged a passage to France on the next tide. She pressed her last few coins into his rough palm, the faint clink of metal barely audible over the lapping water. It was a pitiful offering, but it was all she had. He gave a curt nod and gestured toward the narrow, slick, and swaying gangplank.

A fragile hope, like a candle flame fighting a gale, flickered within her as she stepped onto the gangplank. She had come so far, fought through so much. This narrow strip of wood was more than just a bridge to a ship; it was her final tether to a life she could still call her own.

"Good evening, Madame Delacroix." The voice, calm and merciless, sliced through the swirling mist. It was a sound she knew and dreaded—a sound that carried the weight of justice and the finality of a closing door.

Colette froze; her breath caught in her throat. The gangplank was now a chasm before her, an impossible gap between her and the freedom she had so desperately sought. From the fog, shapes emerged—dark, deliberate, and inescapable. Garrick stepped into view; his silhouette carved from shadow and resolve.

Behind him, a silent phalanx of Bow Street Runners fanned out. Their boots made no sound on the damp boards, but their presence was a thunderous proclamation of her failure. Their eyes gleamed with a grim purpose, reflecting the cold, unwavering light of the single lantern held by the captain.

She turned instinctively, but there was nowhere to run. The fog had betrayed her, cloaking her pursuers as surely as it had concealed her path. Her escape, her meticulous planning, her sleepless nights and whispered bribes—all undone. She had been outplayed, her every move anticipated, her desperation weaponised against her.

As the freighter's engine coughed to life, indifferent to the drama unfolding on the dock. The captain looked away. Colette's shoulders sagged, her fingers curling into fists. There was no escape. Only the cold, relentless hand of justice. And for a heart-stopping moment, Colette considered a desperate lunge, a sprint into the impenetrable fog, but the futility of it washed over her. Instead, a cold, bitter smile touched her lips. "Mr Garrick," she said, her voice a silk thread of defiant weariness, "it seems even the finest nets eventually catch the most elusive fish."

As Garrick's men closed in, Colette offered no resistance. Her silence was not surrender—it was defiance, brittle and burning. The metallic click of the manacles echoed across the wharf; each snap a punctuation mark on the end of her freedom. It was done. The phantom of Paris, the elusive mistress of disguise and deception, had been caught.

The charges would be formidable: grand larceny, conspiracy, and the audacious attempted theft of the Queen's Regalia—a crime so brazen it had shaken the monarchy's inner circle. And though Garrick lacked the ultimate piece of evidence, the spectre of Eliza Beaumont's murder loomed over the proceedings like a funeral shroud. Whispers filled the corridors of power, painting Colette not just as a thief, but as a killer.

Her trial would be a spectacle. Colette Delacroix, once a ghost in velvet gloves, now stood exposed beneath the harsh light of justice. Her grand ambitions—the jewels, the vengeance, the carefully orchestrated ruin of Seraphina Vance—crumbled beneath the weight of truth and consequence...

The Velvet Departure

Word of Colette Delacroix's capture ripped through London's clandestine networks with the speed of wildfire, reaching Seraphina and Aron even before the ink on the official arrest warrants had dried. Aron, still recuperating but regaining strength with each passing hour, found Seraphina in the study, her face a canvas so meticulously blank it betrayed the intense thought churning beneath.

"They've taken her, Seraphina," Aron stated, his voice a low current beneath the buzzing news. "Trying to board a brig bound for Calais. Bow Street Runners swarmed the wharf."

A ghost of a smile, grim and knowing, touched Seraphina's lips. "I expected nothing less from Garrick. He is tenacious, our watchman. And predictable, in his way." Her eyes, however, held a flicker of something unreadable – a complex tapestry woven from grim satisfaction, the lingering sting of Colette's betrayal, and perhaps, a faint, melancholic echo of the brilliant mentor she had once adored. Garrick had at long last caged the viper.

But Colette's capture, while a personal triumph, also signalled an urgent, immediate, and undeniable threat to Seraphina herself. Garrick would have questions. So many questions. He would push relentlessly for further arrests, and despite the protective aura of the Crown she had cultivated, the sheer audacity of the Queen's Jewels plot, combined with Seraphina's intimate, orchestrating knowledge of it, would inevitably lead his gaze, like a heat-seeking arrow, back to her. He had permitted her to be his bait, yes, but he was no fool. He would certainly come calling, and not merely for congratulations.

"It is time, Aron," Seraphina declared, her voice firm, clear, and utterly decisive. "London has served its purpose. We have secured our position, our reputation, and our resources. And the air suddenly feels rather... confined. Too many eyes, Aron. Too many questions on the horizon."

Aron understood. This was the moment they had prepared for with meticulous foresight, the calculated disappearance that always, without fail, followed their grandest scores. Within hours, the grand house in Covent Garden, which had witnessed their triumphs, their sorrows, their most dangerous deceptions, sprang into a flurry of silent, almost surgical activity.

Seraphina dispatched the household staff with such lavish severance packages that it ensured not only their silence but their enthusiastic future loyalty, should she ever reappear? Fine furniture, priceless antiques, and objets d'art not simply draped but expertly packed, their every curve and delicate joint padded and secured, then meticulously labelled for transport to various, nondescript warehouses across the land, their true ownership obscured from prying eyes.

Valuable paintings were carefully removed from their frames and rolled, ready for discreet passage. They meticulously catalogued every piece of silver, every porcelain figurine, and every glittering gem from Seraphina's personal collection, wrapping each in velvet and secreting them away in lead-lined strongboxes destined for underground vaults in Geneva and Zurich. Even the floorboards and wall panels were checked for hidden compartments, for any forgotten papers or overlooked trinkets that might betray a true identity or a lingering connection.

Aron oversaw these final, critical preparations with the precision of a master craftsman, ensuring that not a single personal belonging, no lingering clue, no faint trace of their true identities remained. Letters, journals, even the very inkwells and quills they had used were incinerated, their ashes scattered. The air itself was purged of any lingering scent of exotic perfume or expensive cigar smoke. The house was not just vacated; it was meticulously scrubbed clean of their very essence.

By the time the first hesitant rays of morning light touched the London rooftops, the grand house in Covent Garden stood utterly silent, utterly emptied, a hollow shell. Only dust motes danced in the shafts of nascent sun, remnants of the opulent life that had been packed, sealed, and vanished into the ether...

A Final Glimpse

Before they slipped away entirely, Seraphina felt an inexplicable pull, a need for a final, definitive closure. The next morning, as the magistrate's court prepared for Colette Delacroix's sentencing, Seraphina and Aron mingled with the eager, murmuring crowd. They were masters of disguise: Seraphina, demure in a drab bonnet and spectacles, her elegant posture deliberately stooped; Aron, his usually sharp features softened by a bushy beard and an ill-fitting, threadbare coat.

The courtroom was packed, buzzing with morbid curiosity. When Colette was led in, her head held high, her eyes defiant even in chains, a hush fell, though a ripple of gasps quickly broke it at her brazen appearance. She wore no disguise now, only the stark reality of her defeat, yet she carried herself with an almost regal disdain for her circumstances.

Seraphina watched, her gaze piercing through the layers of the crowd, observing Colette's unyielding pride, the icy contempt she held for the proceedings. A flicker of recognition, a silent acknowledgment of a shared, formidable intellect, passed between them across the crowded room, though Colette could not possibly know her former protégé was present.

The magistrate's voice boomed, cataloguing Colette's myriad transgressions. "Colette Delacroix," he intoned, "you stand accused of grand larceny, the audacious attempted theft of Her Majesty's Regalia, and the most heinous crime of murder, that of Eliza Beaumont."

Colette, however, did not remain silent. As the accusations mounted, her eyes, though still defiant, flashed with indignation. "Innocent!" she cried, her voice ringing with a surprising clarity that cut through the magistrate's pronouncements. "I protest these charges! The jewels were an act of... of daring, perhaps, but the murder of Eliza Beaumont is a vile fabrication! I am no common cutthroat! This is a gross injustice, a travesty!"

The courtroom was stifling, thick with anticipation and the scent of ink and old wood. Colette stood in the dock, her chin lifted, eyes defiant despite the chains at her wrists. The magistrate, a stern man with a hawkish gaze and a voice honed by decades of judgment, leaned forward.

He cleared his throat, then began, his tone clipped and merciless. "The Crown presents overwhelming evidence against the accused, Madame Colette Delacroix. Witness testimony places her at the scene of the attempted theft of the Queen's Regalia, disguised as a palace maid. Surveillance of her lodgings uncovered forged documents, lock picks, and a map of Buckingham Palace marked with precise entry points."

He paused, letting the murmurs ripple through the gallery before continuing.

"Further, correspondence intercepted between the accused and known criminal associates in Paris reveals a conspiracy to smuggle the stolen jewels across the Channel. And though the murder of Miss Eliza Beaumont remains under investigation, the accused's proximity to the victim, motive, and prior threats are duly noted." Colette's jaw tightened, but she said nothing.

The magistrate's voice rose, regaining its full authority. "You stand before this court not merely as a thief, but as a deceiver of the Crown, a manipulator of trust, and a danger to the realm. Your pleas are noted—but they are drowned beneath the tide of evidence."

He slammed the gavel, the sound sharp and final.

"For these heinous crimes, the sentence is harsh, swift, and absolute: transportation to the colonies for the natural duration of your life."

As the gasps echoed through the room. Colette remained motionless, her expression unreadable. But in her eyes, something flickered—not fear, but calculation.

Colette's face, for a fleeting moment, tightened, but then she regained her composure, though a muscle in her jaw twitched almost imperceptibly. She met the magistrate's condemning gaze with an aristocratic indifference that spoke volumes of her unbroken spirit, her lips curling into a faint, almost imperceptible sneer. "Then I shall make the colonies a more interesting place," she muttered, just loud enough for those closest to her to hear.

As Colette was led away, still muttering quiet protests under her breath, her form disappearing into the shadowed corridors of justice, Seraphina felt a strange mix of vindication and a profound, quiet sadness for what could have been. The chapter with Colette was truly closed, its final period marked by the clanking of chains and the echoing finality of the magistrate's gavel…

With Colette's fate sealed, Seraphina and Aron melted away from the courthouse, their disguises shedding like old skins as they hailed a waiting, nondescript carriage. The bonnets and bushy beards discarded in the carriage's footwell, revealing again the sharp features and elegant posture that were their true hallmarks.

Garrick's Empty Hand

Following the conclusion of Colette's damning trial, Thomas Garrick prepared to make his way to Seraphina's opulent Covent Garden residence, where a grim and weary satisfaction settled in his heart. The court ultimately condemned Colette Delacroix, the elusive viper, to a life in the colonies, far from London's intricate deceptions. As he considered the situation, he believed that the city would certainly breathe easier because of recent events, and thankfully, he knew that the Crown Jewels remained secure within the Tower's formidable embrace. Yet, beneath this hard-won triumph, a persistent, irritating suspicion continued to gnaw at him, a restless serpent in his gut.

He had achieved his objective: the principal thief was caged. But Garrick still wanted more answers. More importantly, he still wanted Seraphina. He believed, with a conviction that hardened with each passing hour, that she was far more than just an unfortunate victim in Colette's elaborate scheme. No, Seraphina had been a participant, a co-conspirator who had played him, Thomas Garrick, as skilfully and ruthlessly as she had played everyone else in her orbit. Now, with Colette Delacroix definitively out of the picture, the protective aura of Seraphina's royal shield felt less impenetrable, less daunting. He had given her enough rope to hang Colette; now it was time to see if that rope would lead directly back to her own elegant neck. He was coming for her.

Seraphina and Arons grand house in Covent Garden, already emptied to a mere shell, stood waiting for Garrick's inevitable, fruitless visit. By the time Garrick and his Bow Street Runners arrived the following morning, intent on following up the "lead" Seraphina had carefully laid out for them, they would find nothing but echoing silence and the faint scent of old dust. Seraphina and Aron would be long gone, leaving their life in London – its triumphs, its dangers, its shadowed secrets – behind them with the same calculated precision they applied to every grand design. The city, once their vibrant stage, now held only echoes of their presence.

With grim resolve tightening his jaw, Garrick surged toward the Georgian townhouse in Covent Garden, no longer fooled by its elegant façade. It was a stage—nothing more—for Seraphina Vance's masterful performance. He didn't slow. His boots struck the stone steps with purpose, and his fist met the brass knocker in a sharp, commanding rhythm.

No answer. He knocked again, harder this time—three quick, clipped strikes that echoed like gunshots in the morning hush. Still nothing. The silence was wrong. Not serene, but hollow. Abandoned. A chill gripped him.

"Force entry," he snapped, already moving aside. His men didn't hesitate. The oak door groaned open, not in protest, but as if relieved to give up its secrets.

Inside, Garrick expected opulence. Velvet drapes. Gilded mirrors. The scent of expensive perfume. Instead, he found emptiness. The grand foyer yawned before him, stripped bare. No furniture. No servants. No trace of Seraphina Vance. Just dust motes dancing in the morning light and the echo of his own breath.

She was gone. Garrick stepped across the threshold, his boots echoing hollowly on the polished wooden floors, the sound amplified by the sudden, shocking emptiness. The house was spotless, immaculate, every surface gleaming, yet utterly, chillingly devoid of life. No grand furniture, no personal effects, no lingering scent of exotic perfume or the warmth of recent habitation. It was as if Seraphina, the enigmatic 'Mrs Vance,' the very woman he had cultivated and, to his irritation, been cultivated by, had simply vanished into thin air, leaving no trace but the stark, unsettling echo of absence.

His jaw tightened, a muscle throbbing with rising frustration. He walked through the hollow rooms, his men fanning out behind him, each one a stark monument to her meticulous planning. He checked every nook and cranny, ran his hand along mantelpieces devoid of ornament, peered into empty fireplaces. There was nothing. Almost nothing.

Then, on a pristine white marble console table at the far end of the room, centrally placed as if for an audience of one, lay a single, carefully arranged item. A delicate velvet glove, dyed in a deep, rich indigo, a shade he distinctly recalled Seraphina often wore, its fingers elegantly curled as if still animated by her hand. Beside it, neatly folded, lay a square of heavy parchment, its edges crisp and uncreased.

Garrick snatched it up, his eyes narrowing, a vein throbbing faintly at his temple. The elegant, flowing script was unmistakably Seraphina's. A message. And he knew, with a certainty that chilled him to the bone, that it would not be one of apology or surrender.

My dearest Thomas Garrick,

I extend my sincerest congratulations on your well-deserved promotion to Chief Magistrate of Bow Street. Your diligence is truly admirable, and I trust this new distinction brings you immense satisfaction. It was an arduous task to ensure the proper commendations reached the right ears, but your unwavering dedication made it a pleasure. As for our recent unfortunate encounter with Madame Delacroix, I understand my information proved… invaluable. The world, I daresay, is far more complex than it appears, even for one as discerning as yourself.

Do not despair, Mr Garrick. Our paths are destined to cross again. The game, after all, is far from over.

Yours in enduring admiration,

S. Vance

Garrick crushed the parchment in his hand, its crisp edges digging into his palm, a roar of pure, unadulterated fury tearing from his throat. He had played his part unknowingly in her intricate web. He now realised with a bitter taste in his mouth that she had orchestrated his promotion to the formidable head of the Bow Street Runners, a long-coveted ambition. He had secured the invaluable Crown Jewels, had brought down Colette Delacroix, the phantom of Paris, all thanks to her carefully laid bait. But Seraphina, the elusive "Mrs Vance," the true architect of the velvet deception, had once again slipped through his grasp, leaving behind only a mocking taunt and the chilling promise of a future encounter. The delicate indigo velvet glove, left beside the note with an almost theatrical flourish, lay there, a tangible symbol of her deceit, mocking him with its silent elegance.

He was the chief magistrate of the Bow Street Runners now, at the pinnacle of his career, responsible for the law and order of this great city. Yet, the true mastermind, the brilliant, audacious shadow who pulled the strings, remained free, a phantom in the wind, a challenge whispered across the English countryside, enticingly out of reach.

The hunt, Garrick knew with a cold, clear certainty that settled deep in his bones, was far from over. He would find her. He had to. For the game had twisted yet again, and Garrick, a man of methodical precision and unyielding will, had a score to settle.

As he looked at Seraphina's empty London house, he already pictured the day their paths would cross again. He vowed it would be on his terms.

Chapter 12

Epilogue

The rolling emerald hills of the Cotswold embraced Seraphina and Aron like a verdant, hushed secret. Their new home, a charming, albeit deceptively modest, manor house nestled amidst ancient oaks and beside babbling brooks, was a world away from the grimy grandeur and suffocating pressures of London. A profound sense of relief, almost palpable, washed over them the moment they stepped from their carriage and breathed the crisp, clean air, scented with wildflowers and damp earth. A gentle, unhurried rhythm, a quiet symphony of nature's design, replaced the frantic pace of their old life. They had arrived as 'Mr and Mrs Thomas Moore,' distant, respectable relatives of a somewhat obscure landed family, their carefully constructed backstory as impeccable as their new, understated wardrobes. Their quiet elegance and discreet generosity quickly made them a welcome, if somewhat enigmatic, addition to the local gentry.

And oh, the quiet satisfaction of knowing they had escaped London not just with their lives, but with a substantial fortune meticulously spirited away. This was not merely comfort; it was absolute independence, freedom more valuable than any crown jewel. Their wealth, now safely ensconced in diversified investments, discreetly held caches scattered in unlikely corners, afforded them not only a life of luxurious simplicity but also the ultimate prerogative: the choice. Should circumstance ever demand the resurrection of their old skills, should a compelling challenge or a thrilling opportunity arise, the option to orchestrate elaborate schemes once more is entirely theirs. Their current "gentlefolk" lifestyle in the Cotswolds was no pretence of poverty, but a deliberate, strategic choice, a tranquil haven they could afford a hundred times over, a testament to their enduring ingenuity and foresight.

Seraphina, shedding the elaborate social intrigues and the constant vigilance demanded by the capital, embraced the simpler charms of country life with surprising ease. She revelled in the intoxicating relief of not having to continually scan her surroundings for threats, escaping the need to second guess every treacherous turn in the dangerous dance that was London. Her wit, once a tool of calculated charm, now glinted with genuine amusement as she hosted her intimate garden parties. She contributed generously and anonymously to the village church and various local charities, finding a quiet gratification in genuine benevolence. She spoke with newfound enthusiasm about the merits of rare breeds of Cotswold sheep, the delicate art of preserving summer jams, and the intricate patterns of local needlework, her hands, once deft at picking locks and forging documents, now finding solace in the mundane.

Aron moved through their new Cotswold manor with a quiet competence, his footsteps light yet purposeful on the polished flagstones. He was the unseen hand guiding the estate, ensuring the ledgers balanced with meticulous precision, the staff operated with a harmonious efficiency, and the gardens blossomed under watchful care.

He would often find Seraphina sketching by the window, or lost in a book by the fire, and a cup of precisely brewed tea, or a warming glass of sherry, would appear silently at her elbow. He listened intently to her musings on local flora or the latest village gossip, offering a calm, steady gaze that always seemed to say, "I am here." In his presence, the slight tension that sometimes lingered around Seraphina's shoulders would visibly ease.

When a particularly vibrant sunset painted the rolling hills in hues of violet and gold, he would subtly draw her attention to it, sharing the moment without a word. And sometimes, in the quiet evenings, as the fire crackled and the only sound was the rustle of a turning page, Seraphina would catch herself smiling, a genuine, unburdened smile, something she realised hadn't come easily in the frantic years of London. The sharp edges of past deceptions, the sting of a certain betrayal, no longer pricked with the same insistent pain. Instead, a deep, pervasive contentment settled over her, as comforting and reliable as the distant chime of the grandfather clock in the hall. This new, unburdened existence was built on the sturdy foundation of her wealth, quietly generating its own secure hum in various banks and ledgers.

Yet, the instincts of her former life, honed through years of intricate deception and brilliant orchestration, ran too deep to be entirely quelled. Seraphina's mind, accustomed to the delicate dance of illusion and the thrilling precision of the long con, found new, unsuspecting canvases in the seemingly innocent, gossipy world of the Cotswold elite.

The tranquil veneer of rural life merely provided a fresh stage for her unparalleled talents.

The local squire, a blustering, red-faced man desperate to secure a prestigious marriage for his rather plain, yet surprisingly well-endowed daughter, found himself subtly guided towards a shockingly advantageous match. Seraphina, over a series of exquisitely catered tea parties and ostensibly casual country walks, had meticulously orchestrated the introduction to a handsome 'nephew' of a minor noble house – a nephew who, of course, was Aron's latest, impeccably trained henchman, groomed to perfection for the role.

The dowry, a truly substantial sum intended to secure the family's future and elevate their standing, would, through Seraphina's ingenious manoeuvres, find its way into her ever-growing coffers. Not through crude, traceable transfers, but via a bewildering series of untraceable bills of exchange, carefully laundered through discreet overseas trading companies in Amsterdam and the burgeoning cotton exchanges of Manchester, and ultimately funnelled into a complex network of corporations registered in the nascent colonial ventures. The squire, delighted by his daughter's surprisingly beneficial match and distracted by the pomp of the wedding arrangements, remained blissfully none the wiser, and his daughter, quite content in her new, surprisingly happy marriage, never once suspected the intricate financial currents flowing beneath her newfound domestic bliss.

Then there was the dowager duchess, a formidable matriarch draped in faded lace, lamenting the loss of a treasured heirloom – a magnificent emerald and diamond family brooch believed stolen years ago during a less vigilant period. Seraphina, over the course of several sympathetic visits and profound expressions of shared sorrow, delicately planted seeds of hope. Days later, the duchess was miraculously reunited with a near-perfect replica, 'discovered' by a reputable antiquarian Seraphina had discreetly cultivated through a series of anonymous, substantial commissions. The original, of course, was already safely in Seraphina's vault, awaiting its next transformation. Overjoyed and convinced of Seraphina's keen eye and profound understanding of antiquities, the duchess rewarded her with a truly generous donation to her newly established local charity for impoverished farmers. This charity's accounts, naturally, Seraphina managed with her characteristic flair for "creative" accounting.

Beyond the matrimonial and antique-related endeavours, Seraphina's mind, ever-active, found new avenues for her peculiar genius within the seemingly placid rhythm of Cotswold society.

The Indebted Landowner and the 'Benevolent' Loan.

There was the case of Sir Alistair Darling, a perpetually indebted landowner whose ancestral estate, Darlington Manor, was crumbling around him. He was a man of excellent breeding but abysmal financial sense, perpetually on the verge of losing everything. Seraphina, through carefully cultivated conversations at local fetes and charity bazaars, came to understand the true depth of his predicament.

Rather than overtly preying on his distress, she approached him with the utmost discretion and a façade of pure benevolence. She suggested a "consortium of concerned neighbours" *(a consortium that, in reality, consisted solely of Seraphina's discreetly managed funds)* could offer him a remarkably generous loan. The terms were superficially favourable, ensuring Sir Alistair could keep his home and retain his dignity. However, buried deep within the convoluted legal language, drafted by a seemingly reputable London solicitor (a man long in Seraphina's employ), were clauses that allowed for future "consultation" on estate management decisions, particularly regarding mineral rights and timber sales.

Over time, these seemingly innocuous consultations would grant Seraphina de facto control over valuable resources on his land, ensuring a steady, untraceable income stream that far outweighed the initial loan, leaving Sir Alistair grateful for her "generosity" and oblivious to the quiet stripping of his estate's true value.

The 'Unfortunate' Investment and the Hidden Gem.

Lady Harlow, a notoriously stingy but immensely wealthy widow, was known for her obsession with her sprawling collection of rare orchids. Seraphina, feigning a shared passion, cultivated a close friendship. One afternoon, amidst a discussion of new hothouse innovations, Seraphina subtly introduced the idea of a particularly lucrative, yet entirely fictitious, investment opportunity in a burgeoning tea trade with the East. She presented it as an exclusive, high-yield venture, appealing directly to Lady Harlow's avarice.

Lady Harlow, despite her usual frugality, invested a significant sum. As expected, the "investment" soon ran into "unforeseen difficulties" and was on the verge of collapse. Seraphina, feigning deep distress on Lady Harlow's behalf, then offered a solution: a desperate 'friend' in financial straits was willing to part with a truly exquisite, hitherto uncatalogued emerald, ostensibly a family heirloom, at a fraction of its true value to cover an urgent debt. Lady Harlow, seeing an opportunity to recoup some of her losses and acquire a genuine treasure, snapped up the emerald.

The "friend" was, of course, Aron in disguise, the "heirloom" was a perfectly crafted replica, and the substantial sum Lady Harlow paid flowed directly into Seraphina's accounts, offsetting the initial loss from the "tea investment." Of course, Lady Harlow was left with a beautiful, albeit worthless, emerald and a sense of cleverness in a difficult situation.

In a more daring move, Seraphina once exploited the death of a notoriously reclusive and eccentric local baron, Lord Cuthbert, who died without clear heirs or a publicly known will. Whispers of vast hidden fortunes and distant, impoverished relatives abounded. Seraphina, through diligent research (and perhaps a little judicious eavesdropping), identified a distant, struggling cousin, a young man of moral character but dire financial straits, as the most plausible legitimate heir.

Using her unparalleled skills in forgery and her network of discreet contacts, she "discovered" a meticulously crafted, perfectly aged will tucked away in a hidden compartment of the baron's study, legitimising the cousin as the primary beneficiary.

The local solicitors, after much deliberation and examination, deemed it authentic. The grateful cousin, now immensely wealthy, was subtly guided by Seraphina's "wise counsel" into retaining her preferred legal and financial advisors *(all of whom provided significant kickbacks to Seraphina)*, and also made a substantial "thank you" gift to a newly formed historical preservation society – another one of Seraphina's charitable fronts.

The true heirs, scattered and unknown, remained blissfully unaware, and the cousin, forever indebted to Seraphina's shrewdness, ensured her continued influence and a steady flow of discreet payments for her ongoing "guidance."

Seraphina conducted each venture with almost artistic discretion, cloaking it in impeccable social graces and an untarnished reputation for genuine benevolence.

These were not the grand, audacious heists of her past, but subtle, almost imperceptible manipulations; each one a miniature masterpiece of social engineering. They provided not only a continued influx of wealth, neatly laundered through carefully managed charitable donations and legitimate-seeming transactions, but also, and perhaps more importantly, a quiet, intellectual satisfaction.

Seraphina wasn't merely acquiring money; she was demonstrating, to herself above all others, that her unique brand of genius transcended the murky underbelly of London's criminal world.

Here, among the rolling emerald hills of the Cotswolds, Seraphina Vance found the perfect canvas for her artistry. With a whisper and a smile, she could weave the genteel rituals of country society into a lucrative ballet—everyone enriched, everyone charmed, and none the wiser to the velvet-gloved hand that had so deftly orchestrated their fortunes. The Cotswolds, with its honeyed stone and quiet pride, proved fertile ground for Seraphina's singular harvest. And she didn't just deceive—she delighted.

Each scheme grew more elaborate, more tailored, a bespoke illusion crafted to flatter the vanities and appetites of the local gentry. Contracts were signed, heirlooms recovered, reputations restored—all with just enough mystery to leave a lingering thrill.

Then, days later, the calling card would appear. Not a signature. Not a threat. But a single velvet glove—left with surgical precision. On a polished mahogany desk beneath a freshly inked agreement. On a velvet cushion where a "lost" jewel had miraculously reappeared. Sometimes indigo. Sometimes deep emerald. Sometimes midnight black.

A silent flourish. A whispered taunt. Proof that the illusion had been perfect—and that its architect was already gone.

The Unfinished Game

Meanwhile, back in London, Magistrate Thomas Garrick, now firmly established in his new role and lauded for his recent successes, would occasionally receive a cryptic, untraceable missive. Often, it contained a seemingly innocuous newspaper clipping detailing a surprisingly large donation to a nascent Cotswold charity, or an article effusively praising a surprisingly successful local match that had brought two prominent families together. And sometimes, tucked within the elegant, unmarked envelope, would be a small, perfectly preserved dried wildflower, perhaps a sprig of lavender, or a pressed leaf, its veins delicate as filigree, from a country lane. And Garrick would know. A slow burn of recognition, mixed with a familiar frustration, would spread through him.

He would clench his jaw, a potent mixture of exasperation and grudging respect warring within him. He had caught Colette, yes, and seen her brought to justice, but Seraphina Vance—the true architect of the velvet deception, the woman whose mind was a labyrinth of brilliance and deceit—remained free, weaving her intricate webs in the tranquil English countryside, forever just beyond his grasp. He had his promotion, his reputation burnished, his future in the legal ranks assured. But the game, as she had once promised him with a knowing glint in her eyes, was far from over.

Then, some months later, an invitation arrived, ostensibly for a different matter, drawing him to a country estate in the heart of the Cotswold for a particularly well-attended afternoon tea, hosted by a prominent local family. He arrived, a man of purpose amidst the gentle chatter and clinking teacups, his mind still on the official business that had brought him. He was making his polite rounds, nodding to the local gentry, when his gaze fell upon her.

She was there amidst the roses and the hushed gossip, dressed in a gown of deep forest green that complemented the verdant landscape, a delicate lace shawl draped about her shoulders. Her laughter, a melodic chime, drifted across the manicured lawn. Seraphina Vance, holding court, effortlessly charming the dowagers and engaging the younger gentlemen with an intelligent wit he remembered all too well.

For a long moment, Garrick simply watched, a cold certainty settling in his gut. The sheer audacity of it, her open presence in the very heart of the respectable society she so artfully manipulated.

As if drawn by an invisible thread, Seraphina's eyes, those intelligent, knowing pools of green, met his across the sun-dappled lawn. A small, almost imperceptible smile played on her lips, a challenge perhaps, or a simple acknowledgement.

He moved, cutting a deliberate path through the murmuring clusters of the gentry, the clinking of teacups and the polite laughter suddenly sounding hollow and distant to his ears. Every instinct screamed at him; every fibre of his being, coiled and ready. He saw the flicker in her eyes as he approached, a spark of recognition, a challenge, perhaps even a hint of amusement. She did not flinch, did not turn away. Seraphina, perfectly poised, a porcelain doll with a serpent's mind, stood her ground.

He stopped directly before her, his shadow falling across her elegant green gown. The chatter around them, though not entirely silenced, seemed to dull, as if the very air had thickened around them. His gaze swept over her face—the subtle curve of her lips, the intelligent fire in her eyes that betrayed the innocence she projected, the unblemished

239

skin that hid a thousand deceptions. He saw the flicker of something akin to victory in those eyes, a silent taunt.

With a slow, deliberate movement, Thomas Garrick reached out. His fingers, strong and unyielding, closed around her wrist—not a gentle touch, but a firm claim. He raised her hand slowly to his lips, his dark, piercing eyes never leaving hers. Then, he pressed a light, lingering kiss to her gloved knuckles, a kiss that was both a caress and a promise of reckoning.

The scent of wildflowers and freshly cut grass hung in the air, but beneath it, something sharper pulsed, something dangerous and unreadable. It hung between them like a drawn blade, glinting in the sunlight. The silence stretched taut as a bowstring. Was this the moment of reckoning? The long-awaited arrest? Or merely the next move in their perilous waltz, a tacit dare to continue the game?

Seraphina's gaze locked with Garrick's—unyielding, enigmatic. A flicker passed between them: defiance, understanding, or desire? He couldn't tell. And in that suspended breath, with the world holding still around them, one truth remained: the game was far from over. And as Garrick held her wrist, his heart pounding, he realised that he no longer knew who held the winning hand....

The End

Printed in Dunstable, United Kingdom